That Bad Woman

Also by Clare Boylan

HOLY PICTURES
LAST RESORTS
HOME RULE
BLACK BABY
A NAIL ON THE HEAD (*short stories*)
CONCERNING VIRGINS (*short stories*)
THE AGONY AND THE EGO (*edited*)
THE LITERARY COMPANION TO CATS (*edited*)

That Bad Woman

Short Stories

CLARE BOYLAN

LITTLE, BROWN AND COMPANY

A *Little, Brown* Book

First published in Great Britain by Little, Brown in 1995

This collection copyright © Clare Boylan 1995

The Stolen Child first appeared in *Writing on the Wall* (anthology), *Present Laughter* (anthology) and *Living*. *To Tempt a Woman* was broadcast on Radio 4's *Short Story* and appeared in *Telling Stories II*. *Edna, Back From America* was broadcast on Radio 4's *Short Story* and appeared in *Telling Stories III*. *Poor Old Sod* was broadcast on Radio 4's *Short Story* and appeared in *Telling Stories IV*. *Confession* first appeared in the *Daily Telegraph*.

The moral right of the author has been asserted.

*All characters in this publication are fictitious and
any resemblance to real persons, living or dead, is purely
coincidental.*

All rights reserved.
No part of this publication may be reproduced,
stored in a retrieval system, or transmitted, in
any form or by any means, without the prior permission
in writing of the publisher, nor be otherwise circulated
in any form of binding or cover other than that in which
it is published and without a similar condition including
this condition being imposed on the subsequent purchaser.

A CIP catalogue record for this book
is available from the British Library

ISBN 0 316 87514 7

Typeset by M Rules
Printed and bound in Great Britain by
Clays Ltd, St Ives plc

Little, Brown and Company (UK)
Brettenham House
Lancaster Place
London WC2E 7EN

For my women friends

Oh, why did God,
Creator wise, that peopled highest Heaven
With Spirits masculine, create at last
This novelty on earth, this fair defect
Of Nature, and not fill the world up at once
With men as Angels.

JOHN MILTON, *Paradise Lost*

Contents

A Funny Thing Happened	3
The Stolen Child	21
It's Her	37
To Tempt a Woman	51
Poor Old Sod	61
That Bad Woman	71
Edna, Back From America	85
Horrible Luck	95
Thatcher's Britain	109
Life on Mars	125
Gods and Slaves	137
The Secret Diary of Mrs Rochester	149
Perfect Love	163
The Spirit of the Tree	177
Confession	189

That Bad Woman

A Funny Thing Happened

A funny thing happened one night at the Empress. There was a woman that didnae laugh. No, seriously. Sandy was away into his Man with the Limp. He hardly had to open his mouth. He looked down at the guddle of red faces, rotten teeth bared, stink of beer and gash scent, unwashed clothing, orange peel, ammonia. He released his grip on them, allowed the tide of laughter to die back to sighs and titters as he hobbled to the front of the stage to deliver a sentimental monologue on behalf of those with disabilities. He took a step forward, squeezed them in his fist again. It was his bad leg and he fell into the orchestra pit. The laughter became a death rattle. As he clambered back onto the stage he cast around him a bitter look. They went wild. Applause rose like a storm of birds and then it rained down on him like ashes. There was a curious moment when he became aware that his cold glance was coldly met. There was a woman in the fourth row who watched him stonily. You could tell there wasn't a dry pair of drawers in the house, but here was this one face, shining solemnly out of the hellish dark, a square, plain face and black, suspicious eyes and beautiful long chestnut hair, a superior being, the one who would not eat from his mucky paw, and with a little twist of his heart he knew he wanted her.

The girl was waiting for him in his dressing room. There was another surprise – more a shock – and it made him laugh his hoarse, sour laugh for which he was famous. She wasn't a woman at all. She was only a wean – a big lass but no more than twelve or thirteen. It explained her blank look. She hadn't a clue. 'What's your name, hen?'

An older woman with the same black, suspicious eyes put her hands on the girl's shoulders and pushed her forward. 'Ida May Gordon.' There was a man there too, shifty wee shite.

Sandy wrote an autograph on a piece of card and handed it to the girl. She took it silently and put it away as if it was money owed. She watched him while he took off his make-up, the towel snagging on bits of bristle. 'Did you like the show, Ida May?' he said.

'Aye, great,' the father affirmed.

Ida May crept forward. Her body was so close that he could smell her skin and he flinched away, not because of her smell, which was of soap and salt, but in case she would smell the beer sweat on him. 'What did you mean about those girls and the clergyman?' When he had

A Funny Thing Happened

explained the joke, she regarded him sternly. 'Is that a commonly known fact?' she said.

Exhaustion descended as it always did after a show; the emptiness, the post-egotistical gloom, the sense of opportunity botched or genius wasted. He sank his face in the towel. Ages later when he looked up again they were still there. He had forgotten all about them.

'She's stage-struck,' the mother said.

'Stage-struck.' The words came out of his mouth as if he was spitting sawdust. What the hell did it mean? A desire for attention? Hardly ever anything to do with talent. The feeling that one only came into plain focus beneath the spotlight, in the slap of applause. There was the other side that you couldn't explain, not to a wee girl, that when the dreadful thirst had been slaked and the crowd had composed you out of dark, you flew above them and they ceased to be worthy of your effort. 'What can you do, Ida May?'

'She can dance,' her mother said.

'Can you dance?' he asked the child.

'She's got a stoatin' pair of pins,' the father said.

Sandy almost laughed out loud as the little girl launched into her dance, which was somewhere between the Highland fling and the verruca. Her strong arms struck out like a Glasgow washerwoman. She trampled and pirouetted. She kicked. It was when she kicked that he saw her legs – a real hoofer's pair of pins right enough, long, with little dimpled knees and slender ankles. Funny

That Bad Woman

to think that a little girl could be grown up down there and still a wee tiddler up top. It was like a boot in the guts when he realised where his thoughts had wandered.

'What do you think?' the father said.

'She's a bloody awful dancer.'

In the pub he began to feel sorry for himself. He had never had luck with women. It wasn't his fault, it was the kind of women he met. The only girls he knew were in show business. They smelled of booze and tobacco. Their hot bodies under painted faces made him think of dolls that had been in the dog's bed. They were like himself, all smiles and no hope, wave their fanny in your face, forget your name, call you Andy or Sandy or any-bloody-thing. None of them had ever called him Adam McArthur, which was his real name. He had almost given up on the whole thing. What a man wanted from a woman was more than sex. It was baptism. To immerse his blackness in her snow. To be dipped and renewed. Ballocks. Men were like bloody dogs. With a mixture of self-disgust and self-pity he sank the night's beer with a whisky chaser.

The things that had amused him earlier now came together in a different pattern. He recalled her curiosity. It was a long time since a female had asked him a question and then listened. He forgot that her seriousness came from incomprehension and saw it again as a kind of aloofness, a supremacy. The long legs, the long hair, the little black eyes that scorned and ferreted were all about him like a spell. It wasn't anything he thought about her, only

A Funny Thing Happened

that he couldnae think of any other bloody thing.

She was there the following evening. 'I could tell you liked her,' the mother said. Sandy had not slept. What periods of daze he had had, the little girl had pestered them. When he looked at her now he felt only resentment. The lassie looked back at him with the same hostility, thinly mixed with expectation.

'What do you want from me?' he said to the mother.

'Take her with you. She's no' fussy. She'd do anything.'

Something about the way she'd said it, he got a shudder. He glanced at the child but she was absorbed at his dressing table, trying out things, like a wean playing houses.

'Is her father after her?'

'Him!' The mother's prim mouth curled in contempt. Already he had noticed Ida May's comic imitation of her.

'What age is she?' Sandy said.

Like all children, Ida May was interested in her age. 'I'm twelve.' She turned to them, ghoulish under a rim of black kohl she had put on her lids.

'Get out of here.' He made a clucking noise when he saw how the two females watched him. By asking her age he had given himself away. He quickly removed his gaze but his eye swept the mirror and he saw his expression, ridiculous, not how you'd look at a woman but the way a wee girl would look at a doll in a Christmas window.

'Get out,' he said again.

'Out,' the mother said to Ida May.

That Bad Woman

The child slid past him out the door. Her eyes were on him until her pale face vanished, so that he still saw them after she was gone, two candle burns on a shroud.

'It's no' what you think,' the mother said. 'I have to do my best for her.'

'She's only a child,' he said.

'She's no beauty,' the mother said.

'Aye, and she cannae dance.'

'She's at her very best. She has to have her chance.'

There was a shift of scenery and a musical finale in which villains became heroes and everyone held hands. In a poignant moment Sandy saw that the girl could be his and that she was the only thing in his whole life that he had ever wanted. Maybe he could do something for her. 'We're off to London next week,' he said, 'then Sheerness.' The relief he felt was so strong that he wanted to weep. He couldn't get over the simplicity, the forthrightness.

'How much?' the mother said.

He was gawping again.

'How much? She's not some chorus girl that's been handed round like a peace pipe. She's useful to me at home.'

'Away to hell,' he said. The woman stayed where she was, watching him patiently as if she had something to sell that no one wanted. Somewhere at the back of his head was the daft idea that he would show her Ida May really was worth something. He had to have her because she had come within his reach. He had to place a value on his

A Funny Thing Happened

desire. By the time the two females left, he had parted with two days' takings and he hoped to God he would never see either of them again.

On St Valentine's Day, 1914, Adam McArthur, forty-nine, alias Sandy McNab, set out for London by train with his company and Ida May Gordon, twelve. Now that he had her, what the hell was he to do with her? He told the company that she was there to stitch stockings or make tea or any-bloody-thing.

'Well, don't do any-bloody-thing we wouldn't do,' the dancers said with a wink and Ida's small black eyes bored into them until they had to look away.

'Are you all right, hen?' He tried to court her.

'I want to be like them,' she said.

When he laughed at her she looked like a plain, anxious wee girl. Most of the time he ignored her but at times her presence nagged him like a mouldy tooth. Partly it was her fault, although he knew she didn't understand. She had about her a sacramental air. She followed him about, deferential and possessive. She had made herself his property. Sometimes when she brushed his collar he felt the sweet, humid draught of her breath on his neck and it was like a small door opening at the top of a stairs in a dream. When they got to Sheerness he told her that they were to share a room.

'I'm no' your daughter,' she said to him when they were alone, to set right the account he had given the landlady.

That Bad Woman

When he kissed her white forehead he got the same choking thrill and disappointment as a boy biting into his first green apple pinched from the orchard wall.

Ida May sat at the dressing table with her broad back to him and her beautiful chestnut hair loose on her shoulders. He came up behind her and put his hands on her shoulders. He looked at her hands on the surface of the wood with its ringworm scars of old bottles and glasses. They were child's hands, restless and stumpy. The nails were chewed and on one finger was a ring out of a lucky bag. Her shoulders felt like a woman's shoulders. They were solid and full of reproach.

'What's up, hen?' He tried to coax the muscles loose with his fingers.

'There should be things,' she said.

'What things?' He pressed himself against her back and let his hands run down her chest. Her breasts were hard and almost flat, with a suspicion of prickliness, like a pincushion.

'Women's things,' she said querulously.

He closed his eyes until her obstinacy drew him back. 'What do you mean? What are you on about?'

'I don't know. Women are supposed to have things, combs and bottles of stuff. You put them on the dressing table and you put cream on your face and dab something out of a bottle behind your ears.'

'Take your clothes off, Ida May,' he said.

She turned her astonished face around. 'What?'

A Funny Thing Happened

'Ida May,' he said hoarsely. 'We are to go to bed together as man and wife.'

'What?'

'Do you know what that means, man and wife?'

'Course I do,' she said without any hesitation. 'It means you fight all the time.'

He laughed at her but Ida May's face was blank of any expression except its normal wariness and cunning. Clumsily he began unhooking the back of her dress. She did not try to stop him but clutched at the front to keep him from removing it.

'Ida May, do as I say,' he pleaded.

'How should I?'

'Because I paid your parents,' he said breathlessly. 'They took money off me. They knew what I meant to do.'

She turned around to him again. This time her face registered pure disbelief. She looked at him so long and so intently that he began to burn. When he could not face her any longer he dropped his hands and looked away.

'Say something,' he muttered.

'How much?'

When he told her, her eyes blazed with contempt. 'You must be made of money.'

'Come on,' he said. 'It's not so bad. Lots of girls like it.'

'I'm no' going to bed now,' she said. 'I'd miss my tea.'

'No you won't. We'll get up again. We'll go out and have a feed.'

That Bad Woman

'If you have so much money, you could buy those things,' she said stubbornly.

He asked her what she wanted. Her stumpy hands moved daintily on the dressing table as she mapped out what she wanted and where. 'Soap and scent and a hairbrush. Lip salve. *Ooh dee toilette.*'

She became excited as they walked by the sea. Something about the smell of salt water always got to dogs and children. She stopped to gaze intently into a cake shop window.

'Would you like a fairy cake or a meringue?' he asked her.

She thought about it solemnly. 'A fairy cake.'

'I knew I wasnae wrang.' He laughed delightedly at the old music hall joke.

She gazed at him suspiciously as she ate the cake, delicately peeling back the paper cup and nibbling all around the burnt serrated edges.

After tea they walked along the pier to the music hall. When they got home she was asleep almost before she got into bed. He thought he'd leave her sleeping until he pulled back the blankets and saw her body. 'Don't make a fuss, Ida May,' he begged. 'For God's sake don't make a fuss.'

She scarcely seemed to wake up, except for a look of mild outrage, but after that she merely sighed.

When he woke in the morning she was standing beside the bed. The sheets were flung back and she looked

A Funny Thing Happened

furious. 'What's this? The good sheets! They're wasted! What will the landlady say?'

'Come here, Ida! Hush!' Her little black eyes watched him with disdain as he attempted to explain about the blemished linen.

'Is that a commonly known fact?' she said.

Jesus Christ Almighty, blood on the sheet! His head hurt. He had drunk too much. He was never any good in the morning. If he was with one of the girls they would have lit a cigarette for him, poured him a dram, done a dance to make him laugh. 'Dance for me, Ida,' he said.

She went to the wardrobe and got her good dress. She changed behind the wardrobe door, either from modesty or to surprise him. At the dressing table she clawed the morning tangles out of her hair. She measured with her shrewd eye the distance from dressing table to door and then, while a shaft of sea light spotlit her through a gap in the beetroot-coloured curtains, she spun across the floor, her square face rapt, her lovely legs rising gracefully and landing with a thud.

Sandy sat on the edge of the bed in his underwear. His eyes felt rheumy with emotion. She was unlike any female he had ever known. She was completely untouched by him. She was like the cat that you kicked and fed and then it lit off across the rooftops. He longed for some pity or some tenderness. He yearned to touch any part of her, her hair or her little thumping toes.

That Bad Woman

The dance ended abruptly. She planted her hands on her hips. 'Are you getting me work?'

He shook his head. 'I'm taking you home.'

When she marched over to him he could sense the ghost of a future waddle in her walk. 'I'm no' supposed to be home till Friday. What's my mother going to say? If I don't get a job on the stage I'll be into service. I'm finished wi' school. I cannae be hanging around at home.'

He flapped a hand at her, not wanting to look at the dejected woman's expression he had put on her face. 'It's only a few years, hen. You'll be married then and have weans.'

She watched him so long and so suspiciously that he thought she was going to ask was this a commonly known fact, but instead she came to him and took his hand. He was moved by the feel of her little hand and thought it was a gesture of appeal but she took his hand firmly and placed it on her breast.

'Aw, don't, hen,' he said.

'Do you no' like me?' she said.

He jumped up quickly and a flash of alarm crossed her eyes but he struck a pose in his vest and baggy drawers and launched into his old dance number. He'd been dancing from the age of ten but there wasn't much call for footwork in his new routine. Anyway, at forty-nine he had neither the wind nor the figure for it. After a brief solo he held out his hands and Ida May joined in. They did a bit of tap and a bit of waltz and then they tried a tango. Any

A Funny Thing Happened

other woman would have been creased with laughter, wetting herself, but Ida May was fierce with concentration. Her feet on the wooden floor sounded like horses' hooves sliding on ice.

At first he didn't hear the banging because of the clatter of her feet but then there was the unmistakable shrill of an angry woman from the floor below: 'This is a respectable house.' She poked for attention with the handle of a broom.

Clutching Ida May, Sandy froze in the classic comic 'caught in the act' stance. He almost put his hand over the wee girl's mouth. The child's expression had not changed, but it never did. She was squashed against his body, her little eyes so close to him that they made a single disapproving dot. His own eyes very near crossed as the dot closed in on him.

'Do you no' like me?' she said again, and he felt the petal pressure of her pursed mouth.

This time he tried to bring some tenderness to the act but when he opened his eyes he saw that she was frowning out the window at the sky.

'Sky's turning murky. I wanted to see the sea,' she told him sternly.

Little black needles of rain hung about their heads like clouds of gnats when they walked along the coast. Ida May had put on her overcoat. Her hands were in a muff. She had wound pipe cleaners in her hair while he dressed and put on her *ooh dee toilette*. Although her facial set was

That Bad Woman

grim Sandy told himself she was blossoming in his company. He had gone out of his way to be nice to her, took her to a fortune teller and she damn near smiled when the woman predicted her name would be up in lights. He told her jokes to pass the time. There was the one about the Glasgow man whose house went on fire and he rang the brigade. The fireman said, 'Och, we're awfy busy, can you pit some coal on it and we'll see ye in two oors' time.'

She rounded on him furiously and he smiled in anticipation of her incomprehension. 'You should wear a tie,' she said. 'Only labouring men don't wear a tie.'

'Is that a commonly known fact?' he teased her.

'And you should shave before you go down to breakfast. I was ashamed in front of the other couples.'

Other couples? He stopped in his tracks, astounded. 'You watch your mouth, lass. You should have respect for grown-ups.'

Ida had her arms folded, legs apart, the classic wifie's stance. 'You can't go to bed in your underwear and then wear it all day. I'm no' giving cheek to a grown-up. You said we were together as man and wife.'

Sandy threw back his head and laughed delightedly. 'You're a treasure, Ida May.' He tried to cuddle her but she stiffened in disapproval. The honeymoon was over. Already she was kicking him into shape like a husband.

On the train on the way home she sat on the opposite side of the compartment, not looking at him. Her

A Funny Thing Happened

stubborn face had the weary set of a woman adjusting to a disappointing life.

'Ida May,' he said, 'there's a man I know at the Empress. He might give you a job in the theatre. It'd only be selling ice cream but you'd maybe work your way from there.'

She glanced down at her lap and smiled. It wasn't for him but he had made her smile. Her pale cheeks flushed and her lashes hid her scathing eyes. There was more power in that puny token than in all the applause he had had in his life. By God he had worked for it, but he had made her smile. He felt weak and balmy as if he had just emerged from a deadly fever. And who was he to say that Ida May would not have her name in lights? The stages of the world were full of terrible dancers. He would go straight to the Empress and sort out a wee job for her. Time enough to catch the train back for the evening performance, pie and a snooze on the train. For the first time in years he was looking forward to the show. A thousand people with miserable bloody lives and he could bring them cheer. The Kent countryside fled modestly past as the man and the girl smiled to themselves, each believing their lives to be transformed.

All the time he was inside he remembered her smile, although he could hardly mind the girl at all. She had been at that age when a lassie changes every time you look at her and he only remembered her in the way a man might recall a visit to the seaside as a child; the clean smell, the biting chill, the pearly light that was somewhere between heaven and a line of grey washing. Through the bars on his window he could see the world, a wee rectangle like a savoury served at a ladies' do. The judge gave him two years hard labour. If he could have given him a heavier punishment, he said, he would have done so. Two years, twenty years, his life was over. He could never go back on the stage again. Music hall was clean. He didn't feel sorry for himself. He regretted the girl, though. The Ida May he had known was gone forever. She'd be a woman now. He doubted if she still danced. When the war came he hoped that maybe she got her chance after all, a job in a factory, good money, a soldier to marry. In the end, he had left her with nothing, but he had her smile.

The smile lasted only a moment and then Ida May had her hard, thinking face on again. 'What would you want me to do?' she asked Sandy.

He leaned forward and touched her hand. 'Ach, nothing, hen. You don't ever have to do anything for anybody again. You remember that. You're good enough the way you are.'

A woman got into the compartment. 'Move over beside your father, child,' she said. 'Make room for me to sit.'

'No,' Ida May said.

'You should put some manners on your little girl,' the woman said to Sandy.

A Funny Thing Happened

'I'm no' his little girl,' Ida May said crossly. 'I'm going to sell ice cream at the Empress. We have been together as man and wife.'

Sandy watched her face first, the set expressions retreating out of it one by one, like lights going down in a theatre, until at last her face seemed dark, although in fact it had gone pure white. He had a habit of noting people's reactions for use in sketches. He recorded then the noise of her heels, the dry tapping like the sound of applause in an empty house, as she hurried off to fetch the guard.

The Stolen Child

Women steal other people's husbands so why shouldn't they steal other people's babies? Mothers leave babies everywhere. They abandon them to foreign students while they go out gallivanting, hand them over for years on end to strangers who stuff them with dead languages and computer science. I knew a woman who left her baby on the bus. She was halfway down Grafton Street when she got this funny feeling and she said, 'Oh, my God, I've left my handbag,' and then with a surge of relief she felt the strap of her bag cutting into her wrist and remembered the baby.

I never wanted to steal another woman's husband. Whatever you might make of a man if you got him first-hand, there's no doing anything once some other woman's been at him, started scraping off the first layer of paint to see what's underneath, then decided she didn't like it and left him like that, all scratchy and patchy.

That Bad Woman

Babies come unpainted. They have their own smell, like new wood has. They've got no barriers. Mothers go at their offspring the way a man goes at a virgin, no shame or mercy. A woman once told me she used to bite her baby's bum when she changed its nappy. Other women have to stand back, but nature's nature.

Sometimes I dream of babies. Once there were two in a wooden cradle high up on a shelf. They had very small dark faces, like Russian icons, and I climbed on a chair to get at them. Then I saw their parents sitting up in bed, watching me. I have a dream about a little girl, three or four, who runs behind me, trying to catch up. She says nothing but her hand burrows into mine and her fingers stroke my palm. Now and then I have a baby in my sleep, although I don't remember anything about it. It's handed to me, and I know it's mine, and I just gaze into the opaque blueness of the eye that's like the sky, as if everything and nothing lies behind.

It comes over you like a craving. You stand beside a pram and stare the way a woman on a diet might stare at a bar of chocolate in a shop window. You can't say anything. It's taboo, like cannibalism. Your middle goes hollow and you walk away stiff-legged, as if you have to pee.

Or maybe you don't.

It happened just like that. I'd come out of the supermarket. There were three infants left lying out in strollers. I stopped to put on my headscarf and glanced at the babies

The Stolen Child

the way people do. I don't know what did it, but I think it was the texture. There was this chrysalis look. I was wondering what they felt like. To tell the truth my mouth was watering for a touch. Then one of them turned with jerky movements to look at me. 'Hello,' I said. She stirred in her blankets and blew a tiny bubble. She put out a toe to explore the air. She looked so new, so completely new, that I was mad to have her. It's like when you see some dress in a shop window and you have to have it because you think it will definitely change your life. Her skin was rose soft and I had a terrible urge to touch it. *Plenty of time for that*, I thought, as my foot kicked the brake of the pram.

Mothers don't count their blessings. They complain all the time and they resent women without children, as if they've got away with something. They see you as an alien species. Talk about a woman scorned! And it's not men who scorn you. They simply don't notice you at all. It's other women who treat you like the cat daring to look at the king. They don't care for women like me; they don't trust us.

I was at the bus stop one day and this woman came along with a toddler by the hand and a baby in a push-car. 'Terrible day!' I said. She gave me a look as if she was about to ask for a search warrant and then turned away and commenced a performance of pulling up hoods and shoving on mittens. She didn't seem to notice the rain. Soaked to the bone she was, hair stuck to her head like a

That Bad Woman

bag of worms. She had all this shopping spilling out of plastic bags and she bent down and began undoing her parcels, arranging them in the tray that's underneath the baby's seat, as if to say to me, 'This is our world. We don't need your sort.' It was a relief when the bus came and I could get out of gloating range but still she had to make herself the centre of attention. She hoisted the toddler onto the platform and then got up herself, leaving the baby all alone in the rain to register its despair in an ear-splitting fashion. 'You've forgotten the baby,' I said, and she gave me a very dirty look. She lunged outward, seized the handle of the pram and tried to manhandle it up after her, but it was too heavy. Sullen as mud, she waded back into the rain. This time the toddler was abandoned on the bus, its little mouth opened wide and loud. She unstrapped the baby and sort of flung it up on the bus. Everyone was looking. Back she clambered, leaned out again and wrestled the pram on board, as if some sort of battle to the death was involved. I don't think the woman was in her right mind. Of course, half the groceries fell out into the gutter and the baby followed. 'You're going about that all wrong,' I told her, but she took no notice. The driver then woke up and said he couldn't take her as he already had one push-car. Do you think she apologised for keeping everyone waiting? No! She inflicted a most withering parting glance on us all, as if we were somehow to blame.

Walking away from the supermarket with someone else's

The Stolen Child

child, I didn't feel guilty. I was cleansed, absolved of the guilt of not fitting in. I loved that baby. I felt connected to her by all the parts that unglamorous single women aren't supposed to have. I believed we were allies. She seemed to understand that I needed her more than her mother did and I experienced a great well of pity for her helplessness. She could do nothing without me and I would do anything in the world for her. I wheeled the pram out through the car park, not too quickly. Once I even stopped to settle her blankets. Oh, she was the sweetest thing. Several people smiled into the pram. When I gave her a little tickle, she laughed. I believe I have a natural talent as a mother. I look at other women with their kids and think, *She hasn't a clue, she doesn't deserve her blessings*. I notice things. The worst mothers are the ones with too many kids. Just like my mum. They bash them and yell at them and then they give them sweets. Just like this woman I saw watching me from the doorway of the supermarket. She seemed completely surrounded by children. There must have been seven of them. One kid was being belted by another and a third was scuttling out under a car. And she watched me intently with this pinched little face and I knew she was envying me my natural maternal gift. I knew a widow once, used to leave her baby in the dog's basket with the dog when she went out to work.

And all this time, while I was pushing and plotting, where was her mother? She might have been in the newsagent's flipping the pages of a magazine, or in the

That Bad Woman

coffee shop giving herself a moustache of cappuccino, or in the supermarket gazing at bloated purple figs and dreaming of a lover. Mothers, who swear that they would die in an instant for you, are never there when you need them. Luckily, there is frequently someone on hand, as for instance myself, who was now wheeling the poor little thing out of harm's way, and not, if you ask me, before time.

I can't remember ever being so happy. There was a sense of purpose, the feeling of being needed. And, you'll laugh now, but for the first time in my life, looking into that dear little face, I felt that I was understood.

When my mum died I got depressed and they sent me along to see a psychiatrist. He said to me, 'You're young. You have to make a life of your own.'

I was furious. 'Hardly anyone makes a life of their own,' I told him. 'They get their lives made for them.'

He asked me about my social life and I said I went to the pictures once in a while. 'You could put an advertisement in the personal columns,' he advised.

'Advertisement for what?' I said.

'A companion,' he said.

'Just like that?' I must say I thought that was a good one. 'You put an advertisement in the paper and you get a companion?' I pictured a fattish little girl of about ten with long plaits.

'People do,' he promised me. 'Or you could go to an introduction agency.'

The Stolen Child

'And what sort of thing would you say in this advertisement?'

'You could say you were an attractive woman, early thirties, seeking kind gentleman friend, view to matrimony.'

I was far from pleased. I lashed out at him with my handbag. 'You said a companion. You never said anything about a gentleman friend.'

Well, I make out all right. I get a bit of part-time work and I took up a hobby. I became a shoplifter. Many people are compelled in these straitened times to do things that are outside their moral strictures, but personally I took to shoplifting like a duck to water. It gave me a lift and enabled me to sample a lot of interesting things. The trick is, you pay for the bulky items and put away the small ones, settle out for the sliced pan, pinch the kiwi fruit, proffer for the potatoes, stow the sun-dried tomatoes, fork out for the firelighters, filch the fillet steaks. In this way I added a lot of variety to my diet – lumpfish roe and anchovies and spiced olives and smoked salmon, although I also accumulated a lot of sliced loaves. 'Use your imagination,' I told myself. 'There are other bulky items besides sliced bread.'

Perhaps it was the pack of nappies in my trolley that did it. I hate waste. It also just happened that the first sympathetic face I saw that day (in years, in point of fact) was that tiny baby left outside in her pram to wave her toe around in the cold air, so I took her too.

That Bad Woman

I thought I'd call her Vera. It sounded like the name of a person who'd been around for a long time, or as if I'd called her after my mother. When I got home the first thing I did was pick her up. Oh, she felt just lovely, like nothing at all. I went over to the mirror to see what kind of a pair we made. We looked a picture. She took years off my age.

Vera was looking around in a vaguely disgruntled way, as if she could smell burning. *Milk*, I thought. *She wants milk*. I kept her balanced on my arm while I warmed up some milk. It was a nice feeling, although inconvenient, like smoking in the bath. I had to carry her back with the saucepan, and a spoon, and a dishtowel for a bib. Natural mothers don't have to ferret around with saucepans and spoons. They have everything to hand, inside their slip. I tried to feed her off a spoon but she blew at it instead of sucking. There was milk in my hair and on my cardigan and quite a lot of it went on the sofa, which is a kingfisher pattern, blue on cream. After a while she pushed the cup away and her face folded up as if she was going to cry. 'Oh, sorry, sweetheart,' I said. 'Who's a stupid mummy?' She needed her nappy changed.

To tell the truth I had been looking forward to this. Women complain about the plain duties of motherhood but to me she was like a present that was waiting to be unwrapped. I carried her back downstairs and filled a basin with warm water and put a lot of towels over my arm, not forgetting a sponge and all the other bits and

The Stolen Child

pieces. I was proud of myself. I almost wished there was someone to see.

By now Vera was a bit uneasy (perhaps I should have played some music, like women do to babies in the womb, but I don't know much about music). I took off the little pink jacket, the pink romper suit that was like a hot-water bottle cover and then started to unwrap the nappy. A jet of water shot up into my eye. Now that was not nice, Vera! I rubbed my eye and began again, removing all that soggy padding. Then I slammed it shut. The child looked gratified and started to chortle. Incredulous, I peeled the swaddling back once more. My jaw hung off its hinges. Growing out of the bottom of its belly was a wicked little ruddy horn. I found myself looking at balls as big as pomegranates and when I could tear my eyes away from them I had to look into his eye, a man's eye, already calculating and bargaining.

It was a boy. Who the hell wants a boy?

'Hypocrite!' I said to him. 'Going round with that nice little face!'

Imagine the nerve of the mother, dressing him up in pink, palming him off as a girl! Imagine, I could still be taken in by a man.

Now the problem with helping yourself to things, as opposed to coming by them lawfully, is that you have no redress. You have to take what you get. On the other hand, as a general rule, this makes you less particular. I decided to play it cool. 'The thing is, Vera,' (I would

That Bad Woman

change his name later. The shock was too great to adjust all at once) 'I always thought of babies as female. It simply never occurred to me that they came in the potential rapist mode. There are some points in your favour. You do look very nice with all your clothes on. On the other hand, I can't take to your sort as a species.'

I was pleased with that. I thought it moderate and rational.

Vera was looking at me in the strangest way, with a sweet, intent, intelligent look. Clearly he was concentrating. There is something to be said for the intelligent male. Maybe he and I would get along. 'The keynote,' I told him, 'is compromise. We'll have to give each other plenty of space.' Vera smiled. He looked relieved. It was a weight off my mind too. Then I got this smell. It dawned on me with horror the reason for his concentration. 'No!' I moaned. 'My mother's Sanderson!' I swooped on him and swagged him without looking too closely. His blue eyes no longer seemed opaque and new but very old and angry. He opened his mouth and began to bawl. Have you ever known a man who could compromise?

All that afternoon I gazed in wonder on the child who had melted my innards and compelled me to crime. Within the space of half an hour he had been transformed. His face took on the scalded red of a baboon's behind and he bellowed like a bull. His eyes were brilliant chips of ice behind a wall of boiling water. I got the feeling it wasn't even personal. It was just what he did

The Stolen Child

whenever he thought of it. I changed his nappy and bounced him on my knee until his brains must have scrambled. I tried making him a mush of bread and milk and sugar, which he scarcely touched yet still managed to return in great quantity over my shoulder. With rattling hands I strapped him into the stroller and took him for a walk. Out of doors the noise became a metallic booming. People glared at me and crows fell off their perches in the trees. Everything seemed distorted by the sound. I began to feel quite mad. My legs appeared to be melting and when I looked at the sky the clouds had a fizzing, dangerous look. I wanted to lie flat out on the pavement. You can't when you're a mother. Your life's not your own any more. I realised now that the mother and child unit is not the one I imagined but a different kind, in which she exists to keep him alive and he exists to keep her awake.

I hadn't had a cup of tea all day, or a pee. When I got home there was a note on the door. It was from my landlord, asking if I had a child concealed on the premises. I cackled glumly at the concept of concealing Vera and staggered in to turn on the news. By now he would be reported missing. His distraught mother would come on the telly begging whoever had him to please let her have her baby back. It was difficult to hear above the infant shrieks but I could see Bill Clinton's flashing teeth and bodies in the streets in Bosnia and men in suits at EEC summits. I watched until the weatherman had been and

That Bad Woman

gone. Vera and I wept in unison. Was this what they meant by bonding?

Sometime in the night the crying stopped. The crimson faded from my fledgling's cheek and he subsided into rosy sleep. There was a cessation of the hostile shouts and banging on walls from neighbours. I sat over him and stroked his little fluff of hair and his cheek that was like the inside of a flower, and then I must have fallen asleep for I dreamed I was being ripped apart by slash hooks, but I woke up and it was his barking cries slicing through my nerves.

He beamed like a daisy as I wheeled him back to the supermarket. Daylight lapped around me like a great, dangerous, glittering sea. After twenty-four hours I had entered a twilight zone and was both light-headed and depressed so that tears slid down my face as I marvelled at the endurance of the tiny creature in my custody, the dazzling scope of his language of demand, which ranged from heart-rending mews to the kind of frenzied sawing sounds that might have emanated from the corpse stores of Dr Frankenstein. He had broken me. My nerve was gone and even my bones felt loose. I had to concentrate, in the way a drunk does, on setting my feet in front of one another. I parked him carefully outside the supermarket and even did some shopping, snivelling a bit as I tucked away a little tin of white crab meat for comfort. Then I was free. I urged my trembling limbs to haste.

'You've forgotten your baby!' a woman cried out.

The Stolen Child

My boneless feet tried an ineffectual scarper and the wheels of the push-car squealed in their pursuant haste. Upset by the crisis, the baby began to yell.

There are women who abandon babies in phone booths and lavatories and on the steps of churches but these are stealthy babies, silently complicit in their own desertion. Vera was like a burglar alarm in reverse. Wherever I set him, he went off. I tried cafés, cinemas, police stations. Once, I placed him in a wastepaper basket and he seemed to like that for there wasn't a peep, but when I was scurrying off down the street I remembered that vandals sometimes set fire to refuse bins so I ran back and fished him out. At the end of the day we went home and watched the news in tears. There was no report of a baby missing. Vera's cries seemed to have been slung like paint around the walls so that even in his rare sleeping moments they remained violent and vivid and neighbours still hammered on the walls. Everyone blamed me. It was like being harnessed to a madman. It reminded me of something I had read, how in Victorian almshouses sane paupers were frequently chained to the bed with dangerous lunatics.

By the third day I could think of nothing but rest. Sleep became a fixation. I was weeping and twitching and creeping on hands and knees. I wanted to lie down somewhere dark and peaceful where the glaring cave of my baby's mouth could no more pierce me with its proclamations. Then, with relief, I remembered the river

That Bad Woman

bed. No one would find me there. Feverishly I dressed the child and wheeled him to the bridge. We made our farewells and I was about to hop into oblivion when I noticed a glove left on one of the spikes that ornament the metalwork, so that whoever had lost it would spot it right away. It was an inspiration, a sign from God. I lifted Vera onto the broad ledge of the bridge, hooked his little jumper onto a spike and left him there, peering quite serenely into the water.

At the end of the bridge I turned and looked back. The baby had gone. Someone had taken him. It seemed eerily quiet without that little soul to puncture the ozone with his lungs. It dawned on me just why it was so quiet. There wasn't a someone. There hadn't been anyone since I left him.

'Vera!' I raced back. There was no sound, and when I gazed into the water it offered back a crumpled portrait of the sky. The child was drowned. This person of dramatic beauty and argument, who could command such audience, make a strange woman fall in love with him and weave out of his infrequent sleep a whole tent of tranquillity, had vanished off the face of the earth.

'Vera!' I mourned.

After a few seconds he surfaced. At first he bounced into view and bobbed in the water, waiting to get waterlogged and go down again. Then he reached out an arm as if there were an object in the murky tide he wanted. He didn't seem frightened. There was something leisurely

The Stolen Child

about that outstretched hand, the fingers slightly curled, like a woman reaching for a cake. He began to show signs of excitement. His little legs started to kick. Out went another arm towards an unseen goal. 'What are you doing?' I peered down into the filthy water in which no other living thing was. Up came the arm again, grabbed the water and withdrew. His feet kicked in delight. His whole body exulted. I moved along the wall, following his progress, trying to see what he saw that made him rejoice. Then I realised; he was swimming. The day was still and there was very little current. He gained confidence with every stroke. 'Wait!' I kept pace along the wall. He took no notice. He had commenced his new life as a fish. 'Wait!' For me, I meant. I wanted to tell him he was wonderful, that I would forgive him all his primary impulses for in that well-defended casement was a creature capable of new beginnings. He did not strike out at the water as adults do but used his curled hands as scoops, his rounded body as a floating ball. He was merely walking on the water like Jesus, or crawling since he had not yet learned to walk. As he bobbed past once again I threw off my raincoat and jumped into the water. I stretched a hand to meet the little waving fingers. A puckish gust strained to sweep him off. At last our hands connected. The simple touch of human warmth restored him to the human world. He began to holler.

I would like to report a happy ending, but then, too, I have always hankered after a sighting of a hog upon the

That Bad Woman

wing. It took five more days to locate the mother. She told the police she had had a lovely holiday at the sea and thought their Clint was being safely looked after by a friend who, like everyone else in her life, had let her down. As it transpired, I knew the mother and she knew me, although we did not refresh our acquaintance. It was the pinched little woman with all the kids who had watched me wheel her child away. She said their Clint was a bawler, she hadn't had a wink since the day he was born. She had no money, couldn't even afford new clothes for the baby and had to dress him in their Darryl's castoffs. She was only human but she was a mother and would take him back if someone gave her a Walkman to shut out the noise.

No one bothered with me, the heroine of the hour – a woman who had risked her life to save a drowning child. It was the mother who drew the limelight. Thousands of women sent sound equipment. She became a sort of cult figure and mothers everywhere could be seen smiling under earphones, just as a year or two ago they used to waddle about in tracksuits. Valium sales slumped as women fondly gazed on infant jaws locked apart in soundless wrath. It was left to us, the childless, to suffer the curdling howls of the nation's unheeded innocents.

Some women don't deserve to have children.

It's Her

'I'm late,' Molly said.

He waited patiently to absorb the clatter of his heart. He lived, nowadays, like someone on a railway line who frequently has to break off conversation while a train passes overhead. Molly watched him guiltily and hopefully. When things got quiet he took her in his arms. *This is hell*, he thought. She nuzzled into him in the way someone does who takes love for granted. He felt for the fleshy parting of her mouth. There was a faint stirring of optimism. They had been given a remission: nine months' worry-free fucking.

The phone rang. Molly struggled free. Women always answer phones. They must be primed to respond to shrill repetition in order to keep babies alive. She tidied her hair back from her face. 'Yes . . . mm . . . yes,' she said to the telephone. Her eyes fixed on him in appeal. She put down the receiver in the careful way a child sets down the

That Bad Woman

pieces of something she has broken. 'It's her,' she said.

Peter took the phone in a rage. It felt like a powerful, useful thing but he knew from experience that it was an old enemy, squaring up to him, reminding him that it was coming to get him. He barked into the machine, 'Yes?'

'You're late,' Joan said.

'While your sense of timing is impeccable.' He kept his voice down, knowing Molly would be stung by his tone.

'I want my money,' Joan said.

'You want my money.'

'Bastard!' Joan's cry flew out into the room where it shook Molly. 'It's not for me. It's for your children. You're breaking the law. I want my money now or you can face my lawyer.'

'Tomorrow. You'll have it tomorrow,' Peter said softly.

'I want it now.'

'I'm posting it now. You have to wait for the post.'

'I don't have to wait for anything. Why do you do this every month? Why don't you make a standing order? You want me at your mercy, don't you? You want to make me beg.'

He took the receiver away from his ear and held it against his chest, as if by hearing his disturbed heart she would know that he was not a monster, he was frail. He had two houses to support. His business, which had always looked on the way up, was getting eroded from the underneath by recession. 'I'll write the cheque now. I'll

It's Her

send it round by taxi.' He restored the piece to his ear. His offer fell off into some empty space. She had hung up.

'What will we do? How can we afford another baby?' Molly was crying.

'It's all right. Lots of people manage.' He was taken aback to think that there might be other men whose lives were dogged by leftovers and webbed with panic.

'I wish she was dead.' Molly crept miserably back into his arms.

'No!' Peter was appalled to hear his thoughts coming out of Molly. He nuzzled at her mouth. It was like trying to burrow back into a dream. 'Let's go to bed,' he said. When they got there he was too exhausted to do anything but lie there waiting for his haunting.

When he married Joan she was unformed, a sketch in outline. Now, she had somehow run beyond herself, become a caricature of whatever she might have been. Increasingly, at odd moments, he found himself preoccupied by the question of when she had actually been herself. If she was nothing to do with him, her straggly blonde hair and sad eyes would have reminded him of a drunk old pantomime dame. But she was his. There was no getting rid of her. She was a leak that becomes a flood, a cut that grows into a gaping wound, a sinister woman who turns into a vampire. She was constantly draining him, siphoning him off, mocking his efforts at recovery. He had no use for her any more. He needed his income for vital, present things. Why couldn't she get a job like

That Bad Woman

other women, or find another man? Was it her life's work to strip him and bring him down? He had never been concerned about money. He was a fairly nice man who cared about emotional things, he liked making love and little children. Now his whole life seemed to be money or the need of it or the demand for it. As Molly's breathing deepened into sleep he found himself propelled once more down a familiar corridor in pursuit of a shadowy image. He tried to recall an ordinary woman, Joan. There must have been a time when he knew why he married her and was happy with his choice. Perhaps it happened in a single hour and he had been out at the time, or maybe she was pregnant and the clear line had been blurred. He had a new little family now. A clean page. He was surrounded by worship and trust. He felt like a man who in a moment of hope and madness agrees to lead a group of refugees through some war-torn country. He had promised them safety when, at his age, he knew that at the end there is only death. Every new thing squeezed at his heart – a late period, a child's fall, a large bill, a telephone call that might be from his ex-wife. He lived with the terror and the relief that his heart would give out and the tender gaping mouths would be left behind.

There came a day when he arrived home to find two men hanging around the house. There was something familiar about them. They waved stiffly and he scowled as he steered the car into the drive. What were they? Bill collectors, bailiffs?

It's Her

'Dad!' one of them said.

He didn't see much of his sons. Joan accused him of not caring about the boys and it was true that when removed from the pity and the irritation that their teenage presence inspired he had not felt much, although he was still touched by memories of them when they were little boys. They were men now. The thought occurred to him that they would be someone to talk to, someone to drink beer with. In a few years they might marry and have children who would be close in age to his. He felt not exactly a lightening of his burden, but a fractional shifting so that it seemed better balanced, less likely to bring him down.

'Martin! Stephen!' He said their names loudly to show he had not forgotten them.

'We have to talk to you.' They followed him into the house and peered out the window at the recent garden and some wobbly flowers Molly had patted into the border. Filled with grown-ups, his new, scaled-down accommodation looked like a doll's house. Martin said, 'It's about Mum.'

'She sent you!' He was foolishly disappointed.

'Chill out,' Stephen sighed. 'She doesn't know we're here. It's bad news.'

Peter felt like a tree struck by lightning. He was being split down the middle. Neither half would be any use to anybody. 'What do you want?'

'We don't want anything.' Martin lit a cigarette and hissed smoke at his father. 'Just as well since you never had

41

That Bad Woman

anything to give us.' He sat down and spread his legs. His genitals in their too-tight casing of denim were annoying. One could just tell that when he had finished whining at his father he would be off poking some woman. And without a moment's anxiety. Peter was still paying for him. Hostilities had now broken out between the two men with the jostling coldness of a ship's hulk against an ice floe.

'Cool it, Martin,' Stephen said sadly. 'Dad, shut the fuck up and listen. This has nothing to do with us. It's about Mum.'

'Wait a minute there.' Peter ignored Stephen. His heart had commenced a slow percussion like a sound effect in a horror movie. 'Martin, you said back there you didn't want anything? Correct me if I'm wrong, but it seems to me that I'm still paying to keep a school bag on your back. If you don't want my money I could use it myself. You're nearly twenty. Why don't you go out and get yourself a job?'

'Fuck you!' Martin said. 'Everything comes back to you.'

'It certainly feels that way.' Underneath his anger, elation was beginning to rise. Whatever awful thing was happening in his old family – crime or drug addiction or madness – he did not have to know. The money he was paying was to buy him his freedom. His anger had inadvertently created a diversion. It had steered him out of the dangerous swamp of his ex-wife's unknown disaster and

It's Her

brought him safely back, as Martin pointed out, to himself.

Molly came in then with the two little girls by the hand. 'I bought a dress,' she said. She was flustered. He knew she meant she had bought an expensive dress, one he could not afford.

'Put it on.' He smiled at her. 'Let me see.' The little girls gazed up at the two huge young men in awe and admiration. When Molly had gone up the stairs Stephen was flexing his great big hands in a way that clearly said to Peter, 'I could kill you if I wanted.'

They couldn't talk now Molly was back. They sat in silence until she came running down the stairs to show off her dress. It was white with little blue and yellow flowers. It was cut like a child's dress, loose and high-waisted, so that her small bump seemed like a natural part of her figure. She twirled around on her long legs. With each turn she seemed to change from a child to a woman and back again. This dazzling display upset the boys. Martin stood up and tugged at Stephen's shoulder. He managed a smile and a wave for Molly and then turned to Peter. 'Goodbye, dickhead.' Catching these sights and sounds, the little girls' eyes rotated slowly, absorbing light and darkness like planets rolling round the sun.

Peter was full of triumph. *She's mine*, he thought. *They'll never get anything even remotely like her.* It sometimes made him morose to think that Martin and Stephen had grown up in a generation confident that women were turned on by men's cocks whereas in his time male arousal was something that had to be camouflaged by force of personality and the dark, but even though he was modest and possibly repressed, he had Molly, he had got her, and the bump in her front was proof that he fucked her. 'You look lovely,' he congratulated her. 'The dress is lovely.'

'Don't you want to know how much it cost?' She was anxious to get this out of the way while his mood was cheerful. When she told him he suffered a soaring expanse of panic. He had not imagined anything could cost so much. Joan always bought cheap clothes, rummaged around in sales and tried to surprise him with the smallness of their price. In fact he had ceased to be surprised and taken it for granted that female drapery was an inconsequential thing, practically given away. Like his sons, Molly belonged to a different generation in which women no longer took it on themselves to efface and economise.

'I'm sorry,' she said.

'No,' he said. 'You should have beautiful things.'

When he had first looked on Molly he had seen her as a fresh start. Where do people get the notion that they can start again? He knew now (he must always have known) that every stone you turn, every box you open, you have to carry for the rest of your life. Increasingly he felt an envy of celibate priests, who had been slipped this information at an early age, who could drift weightless through whatever there was of life, until it had to be returned to wherever it came from. All he could see when he woke

It's Her

each morning was the range of his burdens and the knowledge that he must pick them up and carry them, and that he himself had chosen them. What right had he imagined he had to Molly? Early on, when she returned his interest, the pulsing of blood, the restitution of self-esteem had made him feel that he was being brought back to life after a very long period in cold storage. He had plucked a Renoir from the museum wall. How the hell was he to pay for it?

He deliberately let Joan's payment run late next month to show that she could not control him through the boys, that blackmail should be a clean thing, without emotion. He let a week pass, then ten days, and then he wrote out her cheque. The extra time allowed him to adjust to the financial shock of Molly's spending. When he finally posted the allowance he felt an unpleasant potency. Joan could hurt him but he had the power. The telephone remained mutely uncomplaining. It meant she was afraid. He was sorry for her, but he was glad.

Three days later she phoned. 'Hasn't your money arrived?' he said.

'Yes,' she said. 'Thanks.'

'I'm sorry it was late.'

'That's all right. It's always late. I wanted to talk about something else. I want to see you.'

'Can't you say whatever it is on the phone?'

'Can't we be friends? I wanted to say that.'

'Why?' he said. (Dickhead.)

'Because we're the only ones who know each other.'
'I don't know you any more.'
'We grew up together. We're the key to each other.'
He hated it when women talked like that.

Joan's face was gaunt and her hair was matted. He felt sure she had been drinking. 'What is it?' he said. 'What do you want?'

'I need money.' Her voice was hoarse. 'I have to fix things up.'

'What things?'

'That's none of your business.'

'I have no more money,' he said.

'Borrow some.' Her mouth was turned down at the edges and something was crusted in one corner. There were black rings underneath her eyes.

She's like something awful you'd find when you clean out the shed, he thought, to distance himself. *Some beetle.* 'Molly's pregnant,' he said.

Joan seemed to be in actual physical pain. He had no idea what to do with her. After a minute she shrugged but the shrug became a shudder that went on down through her body as if she was burrowing into herself. The effort left a kind of vapour on the air and when she spoke her voice seemed distant, almost disinterested. 'I'm a judgement on you. I wonder if all this was planned before we were even born; our lives, our deaths. I think that's probably true. If there was any possibility, Peter, that you could

It's Her

do as I ask and still forgive me, you might be all right.'

'I am all right.' He spoke stiffly because he was frightened. 'Molly and I . . .'

'You're just a passenger in Molly's life.' Her dispassionate croak sounded mocking. 'She's less than half your age. She'll be living a different life with someone else after you're dead and gone.'

He could hardly speak for anger. His voice came out as if two hands were tightly clasped around his throat. 'And what are you going to do when I'm dead, because you'll have to make a life for yourself too?' When he left, Joan waved goodbye as if she was still sending him off to earn money every day of her life. 'I'm an interloper on the honeymoon,' her hoarse voice called out after him, 'and you know and I know, old pal, that honeymoons don't last.'

She knew nothing. Peter could not decide if he preferred nights or mornings with Molly. Some of the happiest moments of his life were spent talking to her over breakfast in bed. Her questions were thrown in from some naive, wise, uninformed angle that opened new pages in his yellowing opinions. On Sundays they always had sex and toast and coffee and talk in the accommodating duvet. Afterwards they took the little girls for a walk in the park and let them use the swings and then they had lunch in a place where the children could have hamburgers. His children, the children of an older father, did not have the scratchy restlessness of young people's offspring.

That Bad Woman

He liked showing off his new family, his beautiful wife who was sullenly eyed by younger men. The piping voices of the children made intelligent comments on trees and plants. The pleasure he took in this picturesque group was occasionally dulled by an overwhelming boredom, a longing to sit in the car and read the Sunday papers without interruption, but he made the time go more quickly by playing games, pretending that Molly was someone else's wife with whom he was plotting an adulterous affair. He always found it exciting and was able to flirt with her through the children who had an instinct for this game.

Since his conversation with Joan, he saw things differently. He could not but watch from a distance. In a way Molly was nothing to do with him. The trio of beautiful women his wife and little daughters would become would go on after him. They would live a life he would never know. He became fascinated by this idea and in odd moments found himself wanting to discuss it with Joan. Sometimes he felt that he had already died, that he was a ghost ogling the beautiful world from some weightless sphere.

When Martin phoned to tell him Joan was dead, the shock was terrible. He felt he had been poisoned. He was choking on it. Anguish infected every part of his existence. Why had no one told him she had cancer? How could she just walk out and leave no note? Molly, anchored by her seven-month tenant, tiptoed lumberingly around him, aching for his guilt. But his guilt was for Molly. There

It's Her

was no one now for her to lean on. In regard to Joan he felt a kind of admiration and a profound sense of betrayal. She had stolen a march on him, had thrown away his key.

One night he dreamed of her. She was a young woman with a baby on her hip. Her hair was tied back and she was wearing a dress he remembered she'd had for years, thin cotton the colour of strawberry juice. Her body was strong and had a swing to it. *Full of life*, he thought. He stood very close to her, watching her curved lids and broad, knowing smile. When she lifted her eyes to him she was saying something. Their glance met and the surprise was so great that he woke at once. He lay awake with his heart beating too loud. *It's her*, he thought.

For a long time afterwards he tried to have the dream again, to hear what she had been saying and to catch her expression because he knew that if he could look into her eyes he would see himself. He couldn't even remember what her face was like, but he was convinced that she had remembered him. She had taken the picture with her. Once he had been a hero to his sons. He had no image of the giant that had filled their gaze. Now his new children regarded him in the same way but sometimes there was another look, a look of watchfulness. It was as if they saw that he was a foreigner homesick for a country he had forgotten and bewildered by the new world, but they knew what he could not know, that they would see him through.

To Tempt a Woman

The two old men entered Moran's Fashion House accompanied, unknown to themselves, by the ghosts of their lives. A rich spoor of dung and straw patterned the shop's royal blue carpet in the wake of their boots and there echoed off their insignificant persons surprising bass and alto notes from beer and whisky, from dreams of women that made random raids on the derelict imagination, from liniment and black tea and blood.

Miss Hartigan sensed the spectres before she sighted their human catalysts. She left off the cutting of a good wool broadcloth and rushed forward to defend her stock. 'Do ye want something?' She still held the long-nosed shears. A measuring tape, snaked around her shoulders, seemed there to lay witness to the girth of her chest.

The two old men gazed around the coats and corsets, the boots and bales of cloth, as if they were in a foreign country and all the tribes spoke among themselves in a

That Bad Woman

foreign language. 'Sure we do,' they said. 'We'd like a fur coat.'

She saw them as a couple of bowsies, too addled to know where they had wandered in to. 'I'd like one too,' she sneered.

'We're not buyin' it for you,' they quickly assured her. 'Are you coddin'?'

She eyed the fabric of their overcoats, tweed that had developed a sheen as if something had chewed it.

'Here!' One of them pulled from his pocket a thick wad of dirty notes of money, understanding her look. They studied with interest the set of teeth she displayed then, not home grown but hard and white as lime.

'Mink or musquash?' she smiled.

'What squash?'

'That's like a turnip.'

'We wouldn't go for that.'

'How much is mink?'

When she told them they knew they were not in a foreign country but on a strange planet. 'There is opossum,' Miss Hartigan said.

'Quids?' One old man rubbed his thumb and forefinger together, harsh in his fright. 'Name your price.' She named it and he reacted with ire. 'Do you think we're amadans?'

'Was there not another shaggin' creature on Noah's Ark? Lynx, weasel, badger, stoat?' They tried to help her out.

To Tempt a Woman

She knew that male irritation could quickly turn to fury. She was familiar with the bilious strength of old men. Suits might be ripped and mirrors kicked to pieces. 'There is rabbit,' she conceded. At first she pronounced it as if she would neither eat nor wear it and then she forced some eagerness into her voice. 'It's very popular. Also known as a coney or a fun fur. Twenty pounds,' she added. She waited, suspending her breath until they relaxed into their normal state of unease.

'We'd have to see it on.'

'Would you like me to try it on?'

This suggestion cheered them up. 'God, no! She's not a heifer.' They pointed to a young girl behind a mysterious woman's counter labelled 'haberdashery'. She wore a white blouse with a fretwork of flowers on the collar. Tod Cuddy imagined such a presence in his kitchen, her round little face pink from the heat of stove or washtub. Would she ever get used, he wondered, to the stream where at one point the butter churns were dipped for cooling and at another spot you had your wash and far down, where no one could see, you used the running water for a toilet? He only had a son. It seemed a big thing thirty years ago when the boy was born. Now they couldn't see eye to eye at all. It had been assumed that when he grew up the lad would get married and take over the farm but he only wanted a TV. Since they got it he had done nothing except sprawl at its screen watching black and white pictures of people blowing each other's brains out or having

That Bad Woman

a go at each other in bed, taking longer over it than you'd take to eat your dinner. They spent their evenings in the cold kitchen in front of the telly. Occasionally Tadgh drove into town for chips or an awful thing called a pissa. Tod was too long widowed to think of starting out with another woman but he did nine Holy Hours and went off the drink for the duration, hoping that someone would fall for the lad, knowing it would take a miracle.

It was after this that he met a man called Ned Flavin who was trying to get rid of his daughter. 'Why doesn't she go out and get herself a guy like any normal girl?' Cuddy cautiously enquired.

'Phena's only seventeen. She hasn't got around to that sort of thing.'

'Is she a swank? Is she used to finery?' Tod interrogated.

'Get away. She hasn't a bean. She's a nice little thing. The nuns taught her to make a lovely brown soda. Mrs Flavin prefers a white sliced from the local Spar. Presents it at table as if she cut the slices with the cheeks of her backside.' Flavin's laugh came out as an unhappy growl. He couldn't tell a stranger why he had to get his daughter married. He couldn't mention the letter from the nuns.

Cuddy approached his son that evening and proposed Phena Flavin to him in marriage. The lad did not remove his gaze from the screen but continued trying to catch with his mouth the Tayto Crisps tossed from their bag by hand. 'Do you have any feelings in the matter?' Tod persevered. Tadgh shrugged. 'She's a nice little thing,' Cuddy coaxed. 'You'd want to shake yourself.'

'What do you mean?' His boy now turned from the entertainment, amazed.

'You'd be expected to have a fresh shirt at the ready and to clean your teeth regular.'

'My teeth are clent regular.' Menacingly he bared at his father his durable but unappealing fangs.

'So you're keen,' the father murmured, noting with relief that the screen had reclaimed the lad's attention.

When Cuddy met Phena Flavin he was taken aback. She wasn't a nice little thing as her father had said. The girl was a beauty. There were plenty of females that you'd look at in the town, grand big ones with their figures bursting out of their ganseys, but this creature was of a different order. Perfection sat upon her the way it did on a primrose in a field. 'She could get any guy,' Tod burst out in fright.

'Of course we'd like to see her settled with a nice bit of land, but we wouldn't ask her to do anything against her will,' Mrs Flavin said. 'She'd have to be tempted.'

Tod shook his head hopelessly at the notion of Tadgh tempting anyone. 'We're not short of a bob,' he offered doubtfully.

Mrs Flavin smiled to put him at his ease and offered him a slice of Brennan's bread spread with Spar strawberry jam. She was only half her husband's age but there was a

That Bad Woman

coarseness about her that seemed to infect everything she touched. He couldn't eat the meal, thinking of what Flavin had said about the slicing of the bread. When he was going, the girl got his greasy coat from the hall.

'Are you at school still?' he asked her quickly.

'I've done my Leaving,' she told him.

'I suppose you have big plans.'

'I'd like to go to the uni,' she said, and she blushed.

'Now, miss,' her father warned.

The old men had no ideas about tempting women. Neither of them respected Mrs Flavin's view in the matter. She would probably speak of gin or kisses. In the end Cuddy had the inspiration of speaking to the priest in confession. 'If a man wanted to tempt a woman, what item, failing himself, would render her helpless to resist?' he pondered. The priest answered without any hesitation that no woman born could resist the provocation of a fur coat.

They marched down the main street, grim with excitement, swinging the bag by its waxed string handles. They stopped and laughed out loud as if they had pulled off some daring feat. 'A drink, man!' Flavin proposed. They could hear the fur coat languorously shifting in the bag, inside its undergarment of white tissue.

When several pints had worn the edges off his nerves Cuddy found a question rising in his mind and at last, like a belch, it had to be let out. 'Is it fair on the girl?' He was thinking of having to tell her to bring her square of

To Tempt a Woman

newspaper down to the stream. Would she remind him that this was 1967, that men had landed on the moon and the Beatles were selling in millions? In his mind the fur coat had already imbued her with a glamour that put her out of reach.

'You know nothing about the case.' Flavin rounded on him in a fury.

'What is it?' Cuddy was suddenly frightened. 'What are you trying to tell me? Is she used goods?'

'I've had a letter,' the other old man said bitterly. 'From a Sister Felicity. Did you ever hear tell of a nun with a name like Felicity?'

Flavin fell into a thunderous silence and Cuddy wagged his head from side to side as if making a comment, although in fact it was embarrassment. Nothing more was said. He was shy in matters relating to women. At first he felt a profound disappointment that Phena was not as he had imagined her but after he had taken two or three whiskies he was glad she had some awful bloody secret. Whenever he felt sorry for her he could think about that and hold it against her.

Phena turned cautiously from her task at the table when she heard her father's voice.

'I have to talk to you, miss.'

She could tell from his tone that he had been drinking and when she met his eye she recognised the livid and bewildered look.

That Bad Woman

'I know,' she said. 'I know what it is.'

'What do you know?' her father demanded.

'The letter. Sister Felicity told me.'

'It would be better if that matter was not mentioned at all.'

She could not contain her excitement. 'There's a woman in America, a past pupil from the convent, wants a bright girl to look after her children. Sister Felicity said that I was her brightest star. The woman will pay for me to go to college.'

'You want to go?' Flavin said.

'Oh, Daddy, I do.'

'America!' Flavin spat on the ground and she had to jump to save her shoe. 'Have you no shame? Do you think I don't know what you're at, trying to make little of me and all I stand for? What would people say if a daughter of Ned Flavin hightailed it off to the Yanks?'

'What would I do here?' the girl persisted, although she was shaking.

'Come here to me now.' Flavin spoke more gently to his daughter. 'I have something for you.'

She watched cautiously as he produced the bag. 'Oh, it's from Moran's,' she said in surprise.

He shook the container as if it was a sack of potatoes and the coat slid out onto a chair. It looked improper against the bare wood frame and beneath a baleful picture of the Sacred Heart.

The girl ran towards it, her fingers reaching out to

To Tempt a Woman

touch it, but she held them back because she had been gutting fish. 'Oh,' she said. 'Oh, the Lord save us, that's lovely. Whose is it?'

'It's for you,' the old man said and for an instant, when she smiled at him, there was a bond of love between them. 'Now, lassie, we've got a man for you to marry,' he said quickly. 'Will you take him?' He was afraid of the emotional moment.

She slowly wiped her hands on an apron and put out a finger to the coat. 'Could I see him?'

'No.' He shook his head. 'There'll be no nonsense. You'll meet him at the altar.'

She sat on the chair beside the coat. Her hand went furtively into the pocket and caressed it. 'Where would we live?' she said. 'What would he do to me?'

She knew he would not dream of answering such questions. Already his look had turned to scorn for her foolish talk. She began to cry and the old man laughed delightedly for her hand, still stained with the blood of herrings, had fastened itself into the softness of the fur and would not let go.

Poor Old Sod

A shower of blossom fell on the girl's hair. As she looked up he saw her blue eyes diluted by the light. An arc of satisfaction was laid across her face. Her mouth was open as if to accept a drink.

He prepared a small portion of conversation as carefully as one might set a tray for an invalid. '*Wahlenbergia hederacia!*' His voice trembled slightly. 'Forgive me, an old man's excitement. It's quite rare.' He was a neat old man defended against the spring in a suit and overcoat. At first she saw nothing where he pointed, but when he poked among the sinking cherry blossoms with his stick she crouched down in the grass and the earth was starred with blue just as the sky was blurred with pink. She smiled at him and he congratulated himself. He had made time and had lured her into this nest.

The next time she saw him she tried to avoid him. He

That Bad Woman

had talked a great deal on their first meeting, of music and letters and the despoliation of the countryside, while she stiffened in the tree's shadowy roots. When she tried to stand up his face fell. 'I'm boring you,' he challenged. She denied this politely but a corner of his mouth curled ruefully to accept an insult. 'Tell me to shut my trap. It's not often I have the luxury of female company. Since my wife died . . .' He fell silent and spanked the earth with his stick.

She was a young married woman with no ambition. Every day she walked alone in the park. It wasn't really a park. The land behind a derelict house had a garden run wild and some woodland. Not many people used it and she thought of it as her own place. Occasionally one crossed paths with silent joggers or doggy women clad in sheepskins or bands of small boys scuttling like wood lice.

She saw him beating down one of the pathways with his stiff, jointless walk and his puzzled face pulled about by the air, like an old blind dog, and swiftly aimed her gaze at some other view, but she couldn't help looking back. He was askew with disappointment. He had no cover for this treacherous exposure and he had to suffer her discovery of him more than ever like an old dog, his jaw dropped and his features a map of anguish. She waved and waited for him and he bounded up the hilly walk like a crabbed boy.

'I've ruined your walk,' he beamed breathlessly.

Poor Old Sod

'He's an intelligent old man,' she told her husband. 'Sometimes he's quite interesting.' Although they did not meet every day she got the feeling when they happened upon one another that he had been waiting for her. She told Ben how he rehearsed his speeches in order to have some new piece of information to interest her.

'Sounds harmless enough,' her husband said.

She said nothing. Beneath the inoffensive guise of his old man's body she could feel the iron strength of his will and a force of pride for which modesty was a mask. It was mad, of course, but she felt under siege. In some way, he wanted to dominate her.

Her husband thought she was definitely mad. 'If you don't want to talk to him, tell him you prefer being on your own, or walk at a different time every day.'

'He's lonely,' she told him. 'His wife is dead.'

'Poor old sod,' he said with indifference.

'What is your name?' he asked her. 'I don't know your name.'

'Angie.'

'Angie, Angie, Angie,' he said.

She had heard the term 'a new lease of life' but until now had not known its meaning. It wasn't that her old gentleman had shed a decade, but the quotient of life in his ancient bones soared. His diffidence was gone. He pranced. 'Angel! I shall call you Angel. My good angel!' He reached for her hand. 'My angel of mercy!' She let her

That Bad Woman

hand stay there, and bore down upon a sigh. 'I must tell you an interesting tale . . .' he began.

One day when she reached the park he was standing outside. He was looking at the ground and his face was bitter with frustration. She thought of a child put standing in the playground. Poor old man. Someone had hurt his feelings. 'You're late,' he said coldly. She was so surprised that she laughed.

'I know that I am an old man and of no importance to anyone but I am not used to being kept waiting an hour,' he rebuked.

'I'm sorry,' she said. 'I had no idea you waited for me.'

He forgave her at once, before she had time to say that she would prefer him not to imagine such an arrangement. His arm linked hers like a clamp. 'There is something else I have to say to you.' His voice was playful but harsh. 'You did not tell me you were married.'

'How do you know now?' She vowed she would alter her walk. It was a pity, because she liked walking in the same place, made different by the weather or the seasons.

'I found out from someone else. Your name came up and then someone mentioned your husband. They said you were a devoted couple.'

'I don't like talking about myself,' Angie said.

'No.' He let go of her to turn around and look at her. 'That is your appeal.' He smiled his bitter smile. 'I'm just an old man. When a man's wife dies he knows what it is to be unwanted. Go home to your husband.'

Poor Old Sod

'I haven't had my walk yet.' Resignedly, she curbed her stride to match his pace. He picked a wild rose, blushing lividly at its centre and creamy at its hem, with little glossy, fanged leaves. He hectored her with Latin terms before forcing it into her buttonhole. 'A rose for a rose,' he said, and she felt his sharp old fingers touching her breast.

'You look pale,' her husband said. 'You ought to get out more.' A month had passed and she had not returned to the park.

'It gets a bit crowded in the summer,' she told him.

'Go in the evening,' he said.

She smiled at him gratefully. She loved the way Ben didn't make a fuss. They liked one another exactly as they were and trusted each other completely. 'I won't be long.' She put on a light jacket and went out into the dusk.

The park was different at night. The light went off and the scents came on. She leaned against a tree and felt the damp air, drenched in musk and herb and the heavy fruitiness of rose. She knew every inch of path and had no trouble finding her way, and she could see each shrub and tree in her head as their essence greeted her in the blackness.

'You shouldn't be out on your own at night.' A voice rose above the creak of branches. Something hit her on the leg and she gasped. Two small chips like icicles had materialised in a denser stick of darkness. 'It's dangerous,' the old man said. With each statement, he spanked her,

That Bad Woman

not too lightly, on the legs with his stick. 'You young women have no sense.' His walking aid seemed to have an eye of its own and rapped out a spiteful, unerring Braille as she tried to step out of its way, snapping at branches and tripping on hillocks. The anger she felt was dissipated when she heard the grief in his voice. He couldn't control his disappointment.

'I'm fine,' she soothed. 'You gave me a fright. I think I'll go home.'

He was right, she thought as she lay in bed. She could still feel the affront in her shins. Young women had no sense. Why else had she run like mad as soon as he was out of sight? Why else did her heart still pound when she was safe at home?

After that she went to the pictures in the afternoon. It wasn't as nice as walking but there was the same pleasant sense of solitude. Occasionally she had to move as someone tried to be familiar with her but she was relieved to see how easily other men were discouraged.

One Sunday in autumn her husband bundled her up in scarves and led her out to see the trees changing colour. He was concerned about her. She hadn't told him about her visits to the cinema and he worried that she was growing solitary. He was glad to see her hair blown about, her complexion buffed by wind and air, to hear her laughter as he walked fast with an arm around her, making her run to keep up.

'Ah, the happy couple!' The stick described a rainbow

Poor Old Sod

in the air as the old man emerged from a scribble of trees. 'I've heard a great deal about you.' He thrust a complicated hand at Ben. 'Not from her of course!' A wry grimace for Angie.

'I've heard about you,' Ben grinned at the old man.

'No need to tell me. Boring old fart! I dare say she enlisted your aid on ways to get rid of me.'

'Oh, now,' Ben protested. 'She said you were very interesting.'

The old man grinned at Angie. 'You've got a very nice husband. I can see why you might be devoted.'

Angie touched Ben's hand. 'I am.'

'I said you *might* be!' He waggled his stick at her playfully. 'I'm not so sure.'

'She's quiet but she's deep.' Ben was amused by the game.

'She's deep all right,' the old man said, and he fell silent. Ben saw that Angie looked uneasy. He put an arm around her. 'We shouldn't tease her,' he said. 'She's a sensitive soul.'

The old man whacked the earth so violently that it caused an explosion of dirt and pebbles. 'I have never teased anyone in my life.' The stick reared up at Angie. 'You've been keeping secrets from me.'

'She doesn't have to tell you anything,' Ben said mildly.

'Who was that man I saw you with?'

'What man?' Angie said.

'I scarcely have to describe him to you.' He turned

aside and his jaw worked fastidiously as if he did not like the taste of the words in his mouth. 'Tall young man with a hat. Good-looking fellow.'

'That's ridiculous,' Angie said.

Ben looked at her in calm, good-humoured enquiry.

'They came out of a cinema, wrapped around each other. She was eating him with her eyes,' he said to Ben. 'So much so that when I passed her by, she would not give me the time of day.'

'I never saw you there,' Angie said to the old man.

'Where?' Ben asked her.

'The truth, now,' the old man said. 'Out with it!' He spanked her once again with his stick, lightly this time.

'The Adelphi,' Angie said faintly.

The old man smiled sourly at them. He lifted his hat. 'I bid you good day,' he said. He thought the join of their hands, which had made them look like a single unit as he spied on their approach, now gave the impression of something broken and then poorly mended.

'You don't go walking any more.'

'That business,' he said, 'is over and done with.'

'It's good for you,' she coaxed.

The old man gave her a hostile look. 'Good for you, you mean. I bore you.'

His wife ignored this. She was used to him. 'What about that girl you were so kind to – that young widow?'

Poor Old Sod

'I suited her purpose for a time,' he said stiffly. 'She has no further use of me.' He turned away to hide his smile but his wife only saw the stubborn curve of his back, like the carapace of a beetle.

Poor old sod, she thought with compassion.

That Bad Woman

'Are there any shirts?' Henry said.

'I don't know.' Jude felt vaguely guilty. 'Nora did some ironing this morning.'

He watched her searchingly.

'You could look in the wardrobe as easily as I could,' she said. She did not add that if she looked she would see dozens of shirts whereas he might observe the same view and say that there were none at all. He went away without looking in the wardrobe. She stayed where she was, feeling exhausted. She knew that the purpose of the engagement had been to exhaust her but at the same time that he didn't consciously mean her any harm. She wondered if the thought of shirts had passed his mind before or after the notion of unsettling her. *Perhaps we are just a part of the mad animal kingdom*, she thought, *one in which the male is compelled by instinct to aggravate its mate.*

That Bad Woman

Lately Jude had found a shift in her life. The little clusters of trivia that formed the obstacles to her daily existence now became instead long tree-lined avenues. Each event opened up a vista of contemplation and she would sit for hours before a cooling cup of tea, not brooding, as Henry said, but thinking. For most of her life she had never thought about anything, just put up and got on with, but now the small domestic comedy had become a great drama by deconstruction. There was nothing special about her marriage. They got married, had children and those grew up. Because so little happened to her, she was like a grate that has never been properly cleaned, and over the years the flame burned lower and now there was only a dull glow. Henry every so often flung on a coal, but increasingly heavy-handed so that it only damped down the embers a little more. Quite soon, she thought, there might be the final shovel of wet slack that would put her out. She didn't blame him. She just thought of herself as a heap of grey ash.

The moment this idea occurred to her she ran to a mirror and was excited to see that she *looked* like a heap of grey ash. Her hair was straggled with threads of grey, her skin and eyes were dim and she wore a pile of woolly things that she had put on for comfort. Articles in the magazines would have said that this decline was caused by the menopause or by grief at losing her children, but there was as much relief as grief in the safe passing of the young, and her hours of thinking at the

That Bad Woman

kitchen table had led her to believe that the change of life was a chimera, an excision only of the placation hormone which was necessary to keep the home together for the safety of children, and that she herself was much the same as she had been at seven. 'The point of the change,' she told the mirror, 'is that it does not *happen*. It is merely provoked. One must make the change oneself.'

I need another man, she thought, and then immediately corrected herself. The last thing she needed was another man. What was wanted was a partner for sexual intercourse. She did not think of taking a lover, for she did not want to take him but only to have congress with him, and she did not consider him in terms of love, for love, like religion, involved endless searching and a great deal of wasted time. It pleased her best to think of him as the man who would come and clean out the grate.

She went to gaze out the window at men passing by, interested to see them in the new light of prospective poker. How grim and solitary they looked; hard to imagine any of them lying down and rolling about like cats. One of the men was pierced by her stare and turned around in a haunted way and she laughed out loud, thinking of herself as a strange man might see her, knowing her contemplative face was a bleak and horrible spectacle. Imagine *that* with no clothes.

When Henry came home he was annoyed to find Jude sitting reading. 'When's dinner?' he said. 'I'm starving.'

That Bad Woman

Dinner had been at exactly the same time every evening for the past twenty years and there was a plentiful supply of cheese and fruit and biscuits to keep famine at bay.

'Dinner is at seven,' she said, 'but have some cheese or fruit if you're hungry.'

He prowled around, teasing the dog and lifting lids off pots. She went back to reading Mary Wesley to find out about the kind of women who took it for granted that they would have sexual assortment in their lives.

Begin: the hardest part is the getting out of doors.

Like all old sayings it was rubbish but she did actually make several false starts. She realised, for instance, that the brushed-felt hat in a rusty shade of red, which she had worn for several years, looked like a placenta. And she had picked it and paid money for it. Did older men, she wondered now, adopt a walking stick before it became necessary as an aid, in order to wave something erect around? When she started thinking about this, it was so interesting that she almost did not go out at all. Besides, she had absolutely no idea where to go. In the end, she decided to sit in a hotel lounge where she could continue to think her thoughts and where men were reputed to pursue adventure. She sat quietly in a corner and was delighted to witness a very obvious pick-up. When she got home she cooked a lamb stew with almonds and apricots and coriander. Henry hated it, as she had known he would, and she was surprised by the pleasure she got from unsettling him. He didn't say anything, but sat

That Bad Woman

before his untouched plate, looking exhausted.

Jude noticed that her hair had developed a mild sheen. She took a bag of old jumpers to Oxfam and bought a blue jacket in washed silk and wore it when she went back to the hotel. This time she sat at the bar beside a man. After about ten minutes he looked her way and after another ten he told her she was a nice-looking woman. She felt a strange sense of power, as if she had learnt to Speak a Foreign Language TODAY!

'Can I buy you a drink?' she said and was interested when he reacted in the over-pleased way that women do when men buy them a drink. Phrases drifted past her ear like sea breezes – in town on business . . . lonely existence . . . charming company. She said to him, 'I've never taken my clothes off in front of anyone with the light on. Not even in front of another woman.'

The man looked as if he had seen a vision of God in a burning bush. 'Are you married?' he said.

Afterwards, at home, she could not help smiling. The smile kept winging across her face in the way a plane slices out from under a cloud. Henry watched her in dismay. 'What's the matter?' he said.

She thought how nice it would be to live with somebody she could talk to. When she tried to tell him anything he was always urging her to get to the point. 'I went into town today,' she told him.

'I have to watch the news,' he said.

The man at the bar said he was called Bernard. He did

not reveal his second name, for, presumably, he was married too. He told her she had a very frank way of speaking. He liked frankness in a woman. She said she had run out of small talk, she had used it all up on her children, and the conversational fashion for tact and dissimulation seemed to invest every transaction with disappointment. It was like ordering the cheapest thing on the menu in the hope that someone would urge you to have lobster, but they never did.

'Are you suggesting,' he proceeded with caution, 'that you would actually undress for a strange man – and so on and so forth?'

'On and forth,' she agreed.

Bernard had gone on a rampage of celebration, had ordered champagne and told funny stories, mostly concerning bodily parts and ridiculous women, but she did not mind. Jude thought she didn't really mind anything. It was like going on holidays and not caring where one went so long as it was away. She noted the way he masked his eye to make it harmless, how he caressed, with thumb and forefinger, the little scalloped mat that mopped up seepage under his glass.

'Are you very unhappily married?' he asked her.

'No,' she said.

'But not happy, not really happy?'

'No,' she agreed.

He remained silent for a while. 'I don't understand you,' he revealed then.

That Bad Woman

'Understanding takes a long time,' Jude pointed out. 'I should scarcely have thought we had time for that.'

'It's not natural,' he said.

'What isn't?' She waited hopefully to see if he might have a fetish.

'Respectable married women don't pick up strange men in hotels. It isn't natural, you know.'

'It feels quite natural,' she said. 'Much more so than sitting alone in the house all afternoon and worrying about whether I should make a sauce for the fish or grill it, but of course I do have my reasons. I wanted my body and my mind to keep pace. It seems to me that the relationship is between them now, rather than with another person. They have been on different paths all my life, bickering miserably with each other. I want them to make it up, and then to get on with things.'

Bernard looked appalled, uncomfortable, *uninterested*. 'I'm not really sure I want to hear all this,' he said. 'It sounds to me as if you're making use of me.'

'I shan't forget you,' she promised him. 'I shall think of you fondly. Much more than you will think of me.'

He stood up from the bar rather stiffly. 'I think you should see someone,' he said.

The encounter pleased her enormously. She could scarcely believe the rate at which learning could be advanced – and without undoing a single button. What an abyss of ignorance the whole subject of the opposite sex was to women – necessarily so, since they mostly had

That Bad Woman

limited experience and no yardstick for comparison. Her own age group rarely even encountered men in a business setting. It was unfair, since women were genuinely curious about men, whereas men only desired women. *If I were younger,* she thought, *I would make it my business to establish a catalogue of men, to cross-index their physical attributes and mental attitudes. Think of all the trouble women would be saved, how swiftly they could make their choices, how much pain they would be spared.*

When women accept the physical deterioration of middle age, they are said to be letting themselves go. Jude came to the conclusion that the opposite was true; they were hanging on, believing they had outlived their usefulness and must eat up their pauper's stew of plainness, depression and fear. She thought about this at the hairdresser's after she had told the girl that her hair used to be a nice reddish brown and the girl nodded and nibbled her chewing gum and without any argument gave her back the vivid, sexy head of hair she had had in her twenties.

Men sometimes followed her in the street now, although they had difficulty getting her attention for she was lost in thought. To think that the front door had never been locked! She could have walked out at any time. What had held her? The children? She saw again the avid, unfocused infant eye that had pursued her everywhere in her twenties. The unfocused 'I'. One could do nothing with small children. Then the narrow scrutiny of

That Bad Woman

teenagers, watching like a hawk to make sure she didn't get a bigger slice of life than they did. She and Henry hadn't even been grown up when the babies were born and after that any changes in themselves would have unsettled the young. Children fed on unripe fruit and threw the husk away. It must be a natural order since children always displayed resentment of successful parents. Poor Henry, too, might have been dazed and stunted by parenthood.

'Henry,' she said one day. 'Do you ever wonder who you are?'

He watched her warily. 'I have been acquainted with myself for half a century.'

'Think, though! You are unique. Even your fingerprints are unique in the world. When you die, that set will be gone forever.'

He looked around the room, which showed the neglect of her new introspective life. 'I doubt it,' he sighed.

Afterwards, she heard him on the phone, talking to Margaret, their daughter. 'I'm worried about your mother,' he said.

She braced herself for Margaret's bustling visit, the vague irritation in her tone: 'Well, *you're* looking well.' She loved her children but did not much enjoy spending time with them. Their exasperation made her feel less of a person than Henry's silences, and afterwards she was left worrying that she had wasted their valuable time.

It disturbed Jude to think that when first she had

That Bad Woman

contemplated a change of life, the thing that came to mind was a man. What a tyrant the womb was, always complaining if it wasn't served first. She now considered that it might be just as nice to please the eye. She had developed a new way of looking at things in her mind but knew that her visual perspective was lopsided. She used to take photographs but her pictures came out so cramped and sinister that she gave it up years ago. She signed up for a course and became so engrossed in the study of camera that she almost forgot about everything else. But one day when she was pointing her lens at an arrangement of twigs and blossoms on an illuminated sheet of paper, she was suddenly smacked by a feeling of contentment and, without looking up, she knew it was because of someone standing close to her. For once, she wasn't thinking anything at all. Going for a drink with Alec, going to his flat and going to bed with him just seemed a natural thing, like putting up an umbrella in the rain.

A little while after this, she began to wonder if her husband was having an affair. His whistle, as he dug the garden or read the newspapers, was throaty as a thrush's call. When he came home in the evening he poured her a glass of wine and talked about events of the day. He even paid attention when he made love to her. He even made love to her.

She was glad for him, and glad not to have to worry about him, because she herself was devilishly happy. She

That Bad Woman

was only mildly disconcerted that her discovery of sexual delight had no scientific application. Well, there was one interesting discovery. The treasure she had chanced upon was not a miser's hoard. Those around her prospered. The plants in the garden bloomed. The surly cat lolloped and purred. People smiled at her in the street. Even the children now regarded her as an adult like themselves, instead of a backward child or a doddering geriatric. At first she had been fearful of discovery and then astonished by the immunity lovers enjoy, the fact that no one asked her where she went or searched her pockets for clues. She saw now that they were all living on her luck and unconsciously conspired to sustain the holy fire. *One could go on like this*, she thought, *forever*.

She was admiring Alec's long feet one day when he said, 'Have you told Henry?'

'Of course not,' she promised.

There followed a longish silence in which she withdrew her gaze from his elegant arch and met an oddly peevish eye. 'Do you think that's fair?'

She thought about it. 'Strictly speaking, no, but then it is not fair either that I should have been given this happiness by accident. Henry, too, is happier than he has been in years.'

Alec frowned and she cherished the furred caterpillar curved over his smooth brow. 'Do you think it's fair to me?' he said.

'What do you mean?' she pondered.

That Bad Woman

'It's all very well for you.' A new note had entered his voice. It smacked of woe. 'You have a family to go home to. You can't have everything, you know. You have to make up your mind.'

'I'm not leaving Henry,' Jude said. 'That wouldn't be right.'

'What we're doing is not right,' Alec said very promptly.

'Well, I'm not sure about that,' she said. 'When a cup of happiness is offered, it seems downright impolite to seal one's lips, but that doesn't mean you have to knock over everyone else's cup at the same time.'

'Why not?' said Alec.

'It would be selfish,' Jude reasoned.

'I think you are the most selfish person I have ever met in my life.'

Parting with Alec was painful. She had known their affair might some day end but she imagined it would be upon the threat of discovery rather than any mutual conflict. She was amazed by how much she missed him. It was as if one of her children had died. Diplomatically, she removed her grief from the range of her family and went on long expeditions with her camera, photographing homeless children, high-rise wives, oil-sodden birds. Her pictures still came out cramped and sinister but now she saw that this was not so much a distortion as a point of view and might even be a talent. She began to plan an exhibition.

That Bad Woman

She came home one day to find the whole family waiting for her. She was delighted to see them, intensely glad that she had not done anything that would throw into chaos the greater part of her life's work. But then she saw how silence had settled upon them. She caught Henry's eye and she was shocked by his look, like an old dog tied up outside the supermarket and then abandoned.

'Jude, what's up?' he said.

'What do you mean?'

He shook his head in angry confusion. It was like asking a small, displaced child for its address. 'What are you doing to us all? You've no time for us any more. The children can't talk to you. You've shut us out.'

'It's the change of life,' she said kindly. 'I'll be all right.'

'Of course you'll be all right,' Henry said coldly. 'What about the rest of us?'

And she understood that, without knowing it, Henry was enquiring for Alec too. When a poor mother puts chicken soup upon the table, does the family ask where the hen has come from? What right had she to turn her back on nourishment when they were all of them hungry and only she was privy to the larder? A part of her mind began to hanker after her darkroom, where a group of adolescent substance addicts awaited her inspection in the reddish gloom. Another part of her accepted that she had left a mess and she must first of all sweep it up. She took Henry's hands. 'Nothing's up,' she said. 'But if there's anything you want to ask me, I'll tell you.'

That Bad Woman

Henry shook her off. He knew something was up. Her whole appearance had changed. Her figure was better defined and her step had grown jaunty. He yearned to ask about his shirts but he just gave her a bitter look and walked away.

Edna, Back From America

She went up to the water's edge and peered in. It looked cold. *Go on*, she goaded herself. *Can't be much worse than a cold shower.* She lit a cigarette to feel something glowing other than the cabaret sign on the hotel behind her.

She remembered this place when she was ten years of age – a row of boarding houses in different colours fanned out along the prom like biscuits on a plate. When she got off the train with her dad she thought that this was where it stopped at the end of the world. A donkey in a hat waited patiently to take them to the bottom of the pier. And then back. There wasn't anywhere else to go at the end of the world. All week they ate chips and went for donkey rides and made pies out of the sand. He left her on her own at night but she didn't complain. She wanted to seem *soignée*. *Soignée* was a word he used. She couldn't believe it when the week came to an end. She saw the look of pity on his face, the rueful way his lips soothed the stem of his pipe. She was doing what he called a war dance. He took her back to mum and Mr Boothroyd.

It was all changed now, cabaret hotels and karaoke lounges and hamburger palaces. *Everything's different except me*, she thought. *I haven't changed since I was ten. Nobody wanted me then and nobody cares about me now.* She sighed and threw away her cigarette. She began to scale the blue and gold railing. Behind her a crowd started to cheer.

She could hear car doors banging and a lot of excited noise as the cabaret hotel disgorged its patrons. 'Hell,' June said and she stepped down from the railing.

'Edna!' a woman kept calling out.

What would she do now? She hadn't the price of a hotel room.

'It is! It's Edna! Back from America!'

She turned around to discourage whoever was making the racket. A woman in a fur coat ran right up to her and plucked at her leather jacket with little fidgeting hands. 'Edna!' Her eyes glittered with greed as if she was calling 'housey housey'. She had the kind of face that refuses to accept argument or disappointment and that looks betrayed by a jaw settling into middle age.

'I'm not Edna.' June backed away.

The woman frowned. 'Don't you know me? Muriel!' She put out a hand and took it back again. 'Where's your things?'

'I've got nothing.'

Edna, Back From America

'Your handbag?'

Sullenly June showed her hands in which only a pack of cigarettes was held. She pushed them back in her pockets.

The woman nodded. 'You've come as you went.' She seemed quite pleased. 'Everyone took it as proof when you left your handbag behind. No woman leaves without a handbag, they said. Not unless she's dead. You don't know Edna, I told them.'

'I'm not Edna,' June said. 'You've made a mistake.'

'No I haven't,' the woman said patiently. She wouldn't accept anything.

'Now look here . . .!' June began angrily, but her mind had gone blank. She stared wearily past the woman out to sea. Rain had started and the tide lapped delicately at the little mousey shards. Hell, it looked cold. If she had gone into the water and been fished out the following day there would be nothing to identify her. The woman called Muriel would turn up and swear that she was Edna. She began to laugh.

Muriel watched her warily and then she too started to titter. 'You've not lost your sense of humour, Edna. You always were a tease. Now let's not stand here getting soaked to the skin when we could be home by the fire with a nice drop of Scotch. You still like Scotch, don't you?'

Here was one argument at least that June need not resist.

They were settled around the Tudor style fireplace with

That Bad Woman

glasses of Scotch in Muriel's mock-period house when Ted appeared. 'Ted! Look who's here!' Muriel challenged. A big man, uneasy in his successful suit, studied June seriously but without much hope, as if she was an examination paper.

'It's Edna!' the woman said in triumph.

June liked the man. She felt rested under his lumbering gaze and thought that although he had probably lived with the woman most of his adult life, he understood her even less than she did.

'Back from America!' the woman prompted.

'Edna.' He blew air through his teeth. 'America?' He studied her closely while he refuelled her glass. At last he nodded. 'You'd best stay here until things are sorted out.'

As she fell asleep in a room where everything was in matched shades of lavender, she wondered about Edna, what trick of personality she had to make herself so welcome to Ted and his wife while she, apparently with the same face, had no one. Maybe she and Edna were related. Funny how her dad had picked out this place. Perhaps he had a girlfriend here once and left her pregnant. Men were such bastards. Even Alastair. She'd accepted him without question, she'd loved him and nursed him through his illness. When he died there was only the house and its memories. Then his wife turned up. She never knew he'd been married. Alastair's small wealth had gone to her – a woman he had not seen in fifteen years. She was left with nothing. On the train on her way to this

Edna, Back From America

place where she had once been happy, a friendly youth talked to her and after he got off at his station she realised that he had taken her handbag. She was relieved in a way, for there was now no smallest point in carrying on for another day.

'You've gone arty,' Muriel observed over breakfast.

June said that she hadn't gone anything, she still wore the same style she had adopted in her student days. She had meant to leave early in the morning, to complete her mission at dawn on the deserted pier. Absurdly, she had slept it out. 'Look, I'm not your friend,' she said. 'You've been very kind, but I don't know you.'

The woman looked crestfallen. Then she began to cry. 'I'd know you anywhere.'

'I had nowhere to go,' June apologised. 'I hadn't any money.'

'Is that all?' The childish face dried in an instant. 'You always were too proud.' She sat down heavily. 'Look, love, I've got bad news and good. Your mum's passed on. I'm sorry. It's four years ago now. She left a bit of money for you.'

'How much?' June said.

'She didn't have much. Five thousand pounds. And of course there's her cottage.'

Muriel drove her to see the cottage, to show how she had tended the garden. It was a safe and modest little house, guarded by lupins and red hot pokers. June, who was homeless, had an urge to move in right away. It was like a fairy story. She knew she must make known the truth but she could not bear to break the spell.

It was Muriel's suggestion that she should revert to her old hairstyle. She allowed herself to be led to a dangerously homely-looking establishment where a big woman called Beattie greeted her with wonder before holding her down like a sheep to be sheared. As she gripped and snipped, Beattie talked about the old days. The lives of women had not advanced here as they had everywhere else. It was like a dance in which one changed partners for a brief number of years and when the music stopped, when you reached twenty-four or -five, you stayed for the rest of your life with whatever partner happened to be opposite you. Terry had ended up with Renee, Joe and Sarah had a child who was backward, Bill Ferret, who used to look like Elvis, had gone bald and Sid and Sylvie weren't getting on too well.

'Sid and Sylvie,' June echoed distantly, thinking how well their names got on.

'Beattie!' Muriel warned.

They grew silent, watching each other in the mirror as Edna's face was summoned up under the scissors. Had Edna been abandoned by Sid in favour of Sylvie? Was that why she went all the way to America? Perhaps June and Edna had something in common after all. Beattie cut her hair into a mound of uneven bangs that gave her an

Edna, Back From America

odd, rakish appearance. What would Alastair make of her now? She realised it didn't matter any more.

'There!' Beattie said at last. 'There's your old self for you. All you need now is your old accent. Fat lot of good that'll do you.' And she laughed with a noise like a flock of sea birds scattered in anxious flight.

As Muriel introduced her to Edna's old haunts, June discovered that the village had not really changed at all. It was the visitors to the pier who had altered, demanding an updating of the town's single attraction, which had been the donkey. Alice Cranmer's fashion shop still had slips and lemon twinsets in the windows. Girls tried on pink lipstick in the chemist shop. A small dairy displayed faded windmills and postcards and sold damp ice-cream cones. June liked it. She knew that she must someday leave but for the moment she hung about Muriel watching for clues. 'You won't mind my saying, but I preferred your old style,' Muriel offered. Meekly she submitted to Mrs Harkins who pinned her into an assortment of close-fitting Doris Day dresses and costumes. She had her hair lightened and learned to walk on high-heeled slingbacks. When Muriel ceremoniously handed over Edna's old handbag, with its letters and photographs and shopping lists, June did not receive it as a final clue to the other woman's past, but as the lifting of a cloud of amnesia. Everyone accepted her. The one or two who had glanced at her suspiciously soon embraced her and she thought it was not because they had overcome their doubts but

That Bad Woman

because they needed Edna. She was puzzled by the woman who had fled this simple, rich life. She felt entitled to take what Edna had thrown away.

It was a shock to discover that Edna had thrown away a husband and daughter. She found the snapshot in Edna's handbag, a thin man with a solemn girl of eight or nine. 'Sid and Sylvie, Clipton Pier, 1983.' She read the pencilled caption on the back.

'You wouldn't recognise your little girl now.' Muriel shook her head. 'Sid hasn't changed much.' She gave an anxious laugh. 'Your husband never changes.'

June's attention was on the little girl, a child like herself who could not hold love. Edna had walked out on her own daughter. The thought of it brought tears to June's eyes.

'Maybe it's time you went home, love,' Muriel said gently. 'Ted and me don't want to rush you, but everyone's been notified. They're only waiting for you.'

On the way to the cottage she counted up the signs by which Sid might recognise her as an imposter. Had Edna a scar or mole? Was she eager or reluctant in bed? *I'll make it work*, she determined. *A month ago I had no one. Now I've got friends, a family, and a home. I'll make them want me even if they find out I'm not Edna.* She felt calm.

It was Muriel who was nervous. 'About Sylvie,' she said at last. 'I should have told you. She's no better.'

'I'll take care of her,' June said quickly. She was used to sick people. She had taken care of Alastair.

Edna, Back From America

Muriel sighed. 'They won't keep her in anywhere. Not even that mental place. Remember the time she set fire to the rabbit? She did it to a boy in the last home.'

June drew on her cigarette. 'Why couldn't Sid take care of Sylvie?'

Muriel looked uncomfortable. 'He's been inside again. Got in a fight with a man and left him in a very bad way. It's the drink, Edna. You know that. But he's promised he'll never lay a hand on you again. There was some around here thought he'd done away with you. I never believed that. Well, you have to believe the best of your own brother. Anyway he'll behave with Mother around. She's still a battle-axe, even though she's daft as a brush.'

'His mother?' June raked at her face and hair with her fingers as if a growth of cobwebs enclosed her.

'They threw her out of that Haven place now she's wetting.'

'Sid's your brother?' June cut her panic with reason. 'Then we're talking about your mother too. Why can't you look after her?'

'I'm sorry, love. Ted won't have it. I don't mind admitting I was at my wits' end until you turned up.'

'Stop the car, Muriel,' June said. 'I'm not Edna.'

Muriel tittered excitedly. 'You've left that a bit late. They're waiting for you back at the cottage!'

She tried the door. It was secured by a central locking device. 'Please let me out. I'm not Edna. My name's June Pritchard.'

That Bad Woman

The other woman took her eye off the road to sharply assess her passenger. 'You won't mind my saying, but that new pearly shadow makes your eyes pop.' She returned her attention to the road and her plump foot squeezed the accelerator. 'You should draw your eyeliner out at the edges, like you used to.'

Horrible Luck

The two middle-aged women breakfasted together every day. They had nothing in common except their age. Their relationship was based on Mrs Lemon's familiarity with Mrs Lee's underwear, and Mrs Lee's acquaintance with Mrs Lemon's private life.

'How are you today? said Mrs Lee.

'Horrible,' said Mrs Lemon.

'What's horrible?' Mrs Lee still had an eye on her newspaper.

'Me luck,' said Mrs Lemon.

Camilla Lee generously detached herself from Auberon Waugh to give her fullest sympathy to the less fortunate woman. 'Is it himself?'

Mrs Lemon lit a cigarette and commenced a vigorous bout of scrubbing. 'Haven't seen hide nor hair of himself this past six months.' Turds of ash fell from her gasper and

That Bad Woman

as she cleaned the kitchen counter it was dimmed under a coating of lava. Camilla watched in fascination as the trail of grey ash replaced Frederick's more wholesome trail of brown breadcrumbs. Mrs Lemon began to cry. 'It's this letter.' She rooted in her clothing and handed across a sheet of notepaper. Mrs Lee scanned the childish scrawl. It was about St Jude. It enumerated his miracles and favours and attributed oddly material benefits to his supporters, new cars or houses, a big lottery win. It urged the recipient of the note to pass it on to another. 'If you do not do so,' it unsportingly suggested, 'horrible luck will follow.'

'A chain letter,' Mrs Lee laughed. 'It's just rubbish. Here! We'll throw it in the bin. Have some coffee.'

All Mrs Lemon's luck was horrible. Her husband was violent and her children uncontrollable. The woman was so dazed with sedatives and nicotine that she was a fire hazard as well as a terrible housekeeper. Mrs Lee sometimes wondered why she employed her but Mrs Lemon was both her good deed and her talisman. One needed a good deed to propitiate the gods and she liked having her there for comparison, to think that this was the alternative. She herself had married wisely and kept her looks.

Mrs Lemon lumbered back to the table and sat down, rubbing tears from her withered yellow skin. She leaned forward for the sugar and a bolt of ash detached itself and landed in the butter.

'There!' Mrs Lee said kindly.

Horrible Luck

For some reason the episode bucked her up. It made her count her blessings. Life, as she always said, was not merely a matter of luck but of management and she had managed hers nicely. She worked well that morning, dined with pleasure, but without wine, for she was going to a party. It rained when she was emerging late that evening and there weren't any taxis, but a boy with whom she was vaguely acquainted offered her a lift.

'It's kind of you,' Camilla said. She didn't think so at all. She supposed he wanted something. Kim Taylor was young and beautifully made. She admired the selfish curve of his mouth with an edge of temper on it. Young women would think it sensitive. He had a reputation with women. He glanced at her with his piercing turquoise eyes. *I'm enjoying this*, she thought. She supposed he was anxious to drop her off and be with some girl. This did not make her uneasy. She had her aura too. Mrs Lee was successful and had plenty of money and all men liked that. They drove through the night in silence and comfort, each thinking their own thoughts and well pleased with themselves. She was looking forward to tomorrow and, before that, to her tremendously comfortable bed with dear old Frederick asleep in it. They had no children and she thought this was probably a good thing. Children rarely understood how pleasant and absorbing the lives of older people could be. She had no idea what the boy was thinking. Well, how could she? He turned slowly and touched her cheek as the rest of the cars edged forward at

That Bad Woman

the lights like greyhounds at a starting line. 'You're very pretty,' he whispered.

'Don't be ridiculous,' she said, rather pleased.

She was woken in the morning, as usual, by a series of trumpeting laments like a ship bewildered by fog as Mrs Lemon let herself in and began to unshroud herself of waterproofs. Frederick had gone hours ago, departed at dawn, considerately silent, to make money. The smell of coffee ascended. This was the signal for Mrs Lee to get out of bed but as she rose up on an elbow something very peculiar happened. She rolled over, gave a low chortle and then stretched out her body until all the nerves and sinews set up a humming. After that she got up and went downstairs.

Later in the day there was a moment when she studied her reflection with a new interest. Pretty. It was a long time since anyone had called her pretty. Actually, when young she had been striking more than pretty. The word suggested that its bearer needed no other function than to be. It was a tinkling word. It was . . . absurd. She went out to lunch and successfully snared a year's advertising from a French cosmetic company.

In the middle of the afternoon the phone rang. 'It's Kim.'

'Kim who?' she said, but her heart, fired by a single glass of Chablis, did a silly dance.

'Come to the opera with me. I've got tickets for tomorrow.'

Horrible Luck

'I can't. I have an engagement.' She took a deep breath and added formally, 'Nice of you to think of me.'

'Cancel your engagement,' he persisted. 'I'll call in the morning.' He hung up before she had time to put him in his place.

She could never have guessed how pleasant it would be, sitting next to his composed beauty and listening to the beautiful music. There was a starkly sexual quality to his self-assurance. When not attending to the music he had the knack of devoting himself to her completely, ignoring the haunted eyes of younger women.

On the way home he stopped the car. 'What do you want, Kim?' she said and the young man replied, 'I want to go to bed with you.'

'Don't be ridiculous,' she said again.

He stroked her cheek and her mouth with his finger. Then he sighed, turned back to the traffic, drove her home in silence. She passed the night in a frenzy of longing.

Mrs Lemon's husband came back and gave her a black eye. She sat at the kitchen table and wept. He went away again. Her daughter, fifteen, got pregnant. Howls dimmed the hoover's hum and ash gathered in funereal piles. Sharon fell off her boyfriend's motorcycle and she lost the baby. Mrs Lemon grieved amid the alien cornflakes. The house looked terrible. Camilla thought she should give Mrs Lemon a few days off and get one of those cleaning agencies in to do a really good job, but Mrs Lemon shook

That Bad Woman

her head, scattering tears and the dust of tobacco leaves. 'I'm better kept busy. I haven't been myself. It's me nerves. You've no idea what it's like having a threat hanging over you. I can't get on with my life. I keep thinking something bad will happen.'

Considering the normal run of Mrs Lemon's fortune, Camilla could not suppress a smile. 'Whatever can you mean?'

'It's that letter,' said poor Mrs Lemon in a passion. 'That chain.'

'But I threw it out.'

Mrs Lemon excavated the portable black bucket she called her handbag and fished out the crumpled note. 'You have to pass it on. If I don't me luck will be horrible,' Mrs Lemon said stubbornly. 'If I do, there's some other poor soul's misery on my conscience.'

'Now this is plain foolishness and you know it.' Camilla spoke sternly to her domestic. She made a similar speech to Kim Taylor. He had begun sending letters, silly, trivial scraps of flattery better suited to a dizzy blonde of nineteen than to an imposing woman. 'Kim, I do wish you would stop. I'm married, you know.' She listened hard into the line. 'Look,' she added kindly, 'we could talk about it over a drink.' She put down the phone with a shaking hand. Dear God, he had nearly slipped away.

When he drove her back to his apartment there was the briefly unpleasant sensation that she was losing something of value. It was like watching her credit card slide through a grating in the road. She pushed him off feebly. 'I'm not really used to this sort of thing,' she protested.

'You are sweet,' he said.

'Darling Milly,' he wrote (no one had ever called her Milly – it too blatantly rhymed with 'silly'). 'I dreamed all night of my sweet, delicious nymph. How pretty you looked, all dimpled with bliss . . .'

Of course she did not take this seriously. All the same, the succulent little tributes began to assume a sort of integrity. Camilla was changing. She grew softer. She was so happy that she felt able to dispense this benefit. She could be genuinely nice to Mrs Lemon, for instance, and the poor thing grew less abject, for which her employer awarded her a very nice knitted suit, hardly worn, and some advice. 'You have to take control of your life. It is a mistaken belief that you get out of life what you put into it. In fact, you get what you take out of it. Realise your own value. The solution to all your ills lies within your own hands.' So beguiling was her new womanly charm that Mrs Lemon slavishly pursued her prescription. She got a barring order against her husband, though they sometimes met up to go to the pictures or visited a hotel for sex. She gave up Valium and took up yoga. She asked advice about face creams and once Camilla was touched to see her squirting herself as if to extinguish a fire with her new spray of Joy. 'Here!' she said on impulse. 'Take this one for yourself, Mrs Lemon.' And she gave her a half-full bottle of Calèche.

That Bad Woman

'That one is stale,' Mrs Lemon said. 'And my name is Rosemary.'

Sometimes when she rose from Kim's bed, heavy with gratification and drenched in compliments, she was surprised by her reflection in the mirror, of a tousled middle-aged woman. She expected to see what he described, someone sweet and pretty. And young. In some ways she felt younger than him. She had always been in control of her life but no one had ever taken charge of her. They had not understood the burden a successful woman carries, each day having to don her brittle armour of conquest. He had recomposed her, had braved the daunting battlements to rescue the little princess imprisoned within. She was weary of attainment. She wanted to lie down and be praised for the pinkness of her toes. She felt now like a sugar-icing flower on a birthday cake. That is how she *felt*. But what did she think?

'What are your thoughts, Camilla?' a client asked her during an important meeting.

She tried to compose an expression of intelligence on her face, which had lapsed into an aspect of carnal vegetation. *My breasts*, she realised. *I was thinking about my breasts*. She used to look upon these sturdy organs rather as Mrs Thatcher might, like an advance guard which declared her sex and at the same time avowed that it was not to be trifled with. Now they were heavy flowers that sprang from her ribs, narcotic and exotic. She could never have imagined that breasts could have such personality, could crave and declare. Now she understood the French artists and their models and the nature of the great works that occasionally ensued their alliance; that art might be sex and sex might be art. With an effort of will she brought her mind back to the business of the moment and brought the meeting to a conclusion.

'You are a marvel,' her client told her, 'and you get younger all the time.'

Now and again she had the uneasy notion that she was indulging her body too much. It was getting the upper hand. There was the feeling that it sulked if she gave any priority to cerebral issues. The great explosion of happiness that had accompanied the start of her affair was sometimes overtaken by a dreamlike lethargy. The curious idea came to her that Kim had sucked all the steel out of her body and left behind only accessible flesh. Employing his array of compliments he had filleted her. She was becoming like one of those pallid boneless joints that butchers sell for easy carving. She let her hair grow long and her voice became gentler. When they spoke on the phone it was the merest kitten's mew. Now that she had been made meek she discovered a whole new world of women she had not noticed before, young women with eyes of slate and bulletproof shoulder pads, ever watchful of successful older women, not to learn from them but to discern their weakness. After a long lunch with Kim she found that one of these girls had taken over her meeting. When Camilla entered Amy said smoothly, 'I hope you're

That Bad Woman

feeling better, Mrs Lee.' Camilla felt sorry for the girl and the aridness of her ambition. While she worked she was assailed by pangs of emotion. Gusts of erotic longing swept her off her feet. Sometimes she felt euphoric and full of energy. At other times she was morbid and breathless and obsessive, as if she had spent all day searching the attic for something that could not be found.

'You're working too hard,' Frederick said.

'Nonsense,' she said, and tears filled her eyes.

He put an arm around her and kissed her fondly. 'You're worn out. You're working too many nights. You're getting that demented look career women sometimes have.'

She took a few days off and her languid body wilted into fever. She was unable to eat anything but devoured from her precious hoard of Kim's letters the sugared phrases to which she had become addict. All she had for company was Mrs Lemon, who hitched up her skirt to show off her new oestrogen patch. 'You should try one,' she crowed. 'It gives you back your libido.'

The malady left her weak and abstracted. When she returned to work she found herself increasingly reliant on young Amy. She went to the doctor to find out what was wrong with her. He examined all her lovely parts without remark and then confessed he simply did not know. 'Of course you don't!' Camilla cried. How could he know, for she had only just realised herself. She had fallen in love.

Horrible Luck

She phoned Kim right away. 'I've something to tell you.'

'Me too,' he said. 'Meet me tonight.'

Something had happened during her sickness. She was not as glossily powerful as she had been before. She painted her face with care and it looked back at her anxiously. She had got too thin. She was beginning to look old.

None of this seemed to matter with Kim. 'Darling, I've never felt this way before,' he said at once. Leaving Frederick would be difficult but at least they would not have to live in a garret. Kim was one of the rising young men in his field. They would have a splendid life. First thing, she would get rid of Mrs Lemon and hire a proper housekeeper. Kim was talking about marriage, his turquoise eyes transformed by tenderness. 'Congratulate me, darling,' he said. 'Her name is Heather.'

She would fire Mrs Lemon anyway, get a woman who could do flowers, make decent coffee, launder silk underwear without bringing it to the boil.

Kim thanked Camilla from the bottom of his heart, which was not the bit of his heart she craved. Heather was a pure girl, very young, and *sweet*. He could not have held out without Camilla. 'I picked you with great care,' he exulted. 'It had to be someone whose life was totally fulfilled. Otherwise, I would have felt a shit.'

Mrs Lemon turned up in a coat made up of many small dead animals. Tufts of ash adorned its collar and a musky

That Bad Woman

aroma surrounded her. She was smoking cannabis now. Camilla had ready a small speech of termination. She handed over a cheque first to soften the blow.

'Bless you, Missus,' said Mrs Lemon with an explosion of mirth which scattered ash over everything. 'I don't need your money. In fact, I have a little something for you – a parting present, if you like. You see I've had a bit of luck on the pools so I reckon it's time Rosie gave herself a rest.' She watched with happiness as Mrs Lee unwrapped the package which exploded into a parachute of pink nylon. 'Brighten up your night life, if you get my meaning,' said Mrs Lemon with a wink. 'I wouldn't have the cheek to say this only I'm handing in my notice, but we're of an age and it's meant in friendship. You're giving in to your years.'

Oddly, she missed Mrs Lemon. Two other cleaning women came and went and the effort of keeping house along with the demands of her career got her down. Frederick was right. She was working too hard. Midway through an appalling day she handed in her notice. Everyone was very understanding.

Except Frederick. She came home needing sympathy but he was absorbed in something he was reading. 'I found this. I knew something was up, Camilla, but how could you have been taken in by such rubbish?' His voice was mild, but he sounded shaken. Her heart gave a dreadful lurch when she saw the slip of notepaper. Camilla had the unpleasant but literal sensation of her world turning

Horrible Luck

upside down. The blood vanished from her head and her legs went weak. She had forgotten to destroy Kim's letters.

'I'm sorry, Frederick!' she said humbly, and sank to her knees.

Her husband watched her in dismay. 'Get up off your knees, old thing. Let me give you a good stiff drink.' Gin was ruinous to the complexion but she drank it anyway. 'We must get to the bottom of this.' Frederick's nice old face searched her gaunt and guilty one benignly. 'Now, who on earth would have sent you a chain letter?'

Thatcher's Britain

Ten Hail Marys and he'll phone. She said the prayers slowly, trying to put feeling into them. The harder she concentrated the more the words lost their meaning. *Fruit of thy womb.* Imagine, though, if little currants came out down there. Or pink blossoms that would scatter when you ran. The reality was more devious, things running riot everywhere, unseen.

All day she had heard a baby crying from some other part of the house, like a donkey braying in a far meadow. She tried to imagine what colour it was, black or chestnut or the dry, flat brown of winter leaves. Would his mother give him a bit of bread and sugar to comfort him? Her own mother used to give her her vest to suck when she was desolate. It became a craving, after you were weaned, the taste of your mother.

Two hundred drops of rain and he'll ring. She made an effort to keep track but the blobs of water slithered into

That Bad Woman

each other on the window like drunks at a dance. Wouldn't you think now water was clear as crystal? Lepping with organisms, in point of fact. Every drop of London water you drank had passed through nine people. She preferred to think it had passed through a woman than a man. The way her hand went to the phone and began to dial reminded her of a character she had seen in the pictures, strangling a woman. He did it as if his hands were nothing to do with him. There was a kind of magic in it, though. She just poked the dial and there he was.

'I miss you,' she said.

There was a small chastising silence and she listened hard, not even wishing to miss the sigh as he spoke. 'I told you not to ring here.'

'Will I see you so?'

'Perhaps. Later.'

'Will you want some dinner?' Kathleen coaxed.

'I'll have eaten.' He said it grudgingly, as if she had extracted information under duress.

'It's only that I've been invited to dine with someone else,' she quickly defended herself.

'Ah, well. Some other evening.'

'It's an early dinner. I'll be back. What time will I see you?'

'I'm afraid I have no idea.'

'I'll be back.'

To soften the lie she had told him, as well as to put in the hours until she saw him, she tied on a scarf and went out into the rain. There was a little Italian place not too far away where they treated you nicely if you were on your own and you could get a beautiful lasagne at reasonable cost. Her money was nearly gone, but she would find work now her spirits were improved. On the tube she sat opposite a black woman who clutched a parcel labelled 'Mrs Blessings Okara'. A young rabbi, seated beside her, murmured something to her and she could not quite hear, but it seemed he was advising her that you could buy very good diamonds in Harrods. Her attention was taken by an Indian family who occupied a whole row of seats and she was mesmerised by the glittering painted toes of the doe-like teenage girl. She could not imagine how they saw her. She had no clear picture of herself, having been schooled against the sin of self-absorption, but she was going to see him and she felt her happiness must be plain for all to see, stretched across her like a rainbow.

When she got to the restaurant she looked in the window and there were couples already there, early diners, discussing the menu over a drink. Her elation vanished. By the time she saw him he would be full of a dinner eaten alone or with someone else, consumed in that mannerly way he had, the prongs of the fork vanishing between his lips and then only a vague abstraction of the eye and a faint budging of his chin betrayed that any activity was going on at all. You never saw him swallowing. He had taken her out to dinner once and she knew that she loved him because she ate snails to please him. That was

That Bad Woman

how they got around to sex as well. You would do anything for someone if you loved them.

She went instead to a joint with loud music. Her salad was full of hard bits, red cabbage and brown beans and sweet corn and lumps of onion. The entire nation must be consumed with the state of its bowels, the grub they ate. No wonder they looked undernourished. Rubble like this would go through you like a dose of salts. She was suddenly homesick for the salads back home, a few petals of soft green lettuce, a hard boiled egg with buttercup centre, a sliver of home-cured ham and a sprig of scallion. With her mouth full of red cabbage she burst into tears.

What was it she saw in him? At first it was what she thought of as his Englishness, his beautiful manners and the way he spoke, without a trace of harshness. She had lost her way and looked around for a respectable person to give her directions. He offered her the shelter of his umbrella, 'to protect your beautiful hair.'

'Ah, sure 'tis only old wire,' she mocked.

'Gold wire,' he said. When it was time for him to go he left her his umbrella. 'You can return it when the weather changes.' A gentleman like that would never be unkind to you. She hung his umbrella on the mantelpiece where she could watch it from her bed, a piece of England, furled tautly as a new oak leaf. Every so often she would shake out its folds and smell its good fabric smell and know that she had left behind forever the mean little black umbrellas of home, always busted, the spokes sticking out at all angles so that they lay on the step like a mangled crow.

'Call me J,' he said. She thought of him as Jay, like a bird, but the few notes he sent her were tersely signed with an initial. She imagined he must be something very high up and secret in the government and of course, as he was compelled to mention, he had a life before he met her, all the trimmings. He could not speak about his job and was too discreet to discuss his personal life but she was content to hear him talk about things he liked, good wine, the opera, poems, books, ballet, restaurants where whole sides of beef were carved.

'Oh, I'd love all that,' she said.

'You should have it,' he smiled. There was such happiness in the assertion that she would like to have had it bottled and sent back home as a tonic, only they would have laughed at his accent.

He took her to a restaurant with candles on the table and small silver vessels of flowers such as you'd see on the altar. In fact the whole event had about it the air of a religious ceremony. When the waiter poured a sup of wine J raised it up to the light and twirled it round and then stuck his nose in the glass and swilled a drop in his mouth with a mystical look. Kathleen expected to hear a little bell ringing. 'To England!' he toasted. After he had drunk some wine he grew maudlin. He raised his glass again. 'To loved ones left behind.' She thought first of his wife and then of her mother. As always, she pictured her mother in wellingtons and a man's overcoat, her hands mottled

That Bad Woman

mauve like Swede turnips, her face closed off against the danger of emotion.

She had been shocked when she arrived in London to discover the young Irish people living in derelict houses with broken windows and boarded up doors, paying no rent. She took a room in a house in Notting Hill where there was a respectable Irish family, but one night they vanished and she was surrounded by silent people with amber skin and dark-skinned people who played loud music and addressed their neighbours by shouting out the window. All the women had children and because she had no child they had nothing to say to her but she thought that inside they must feel the same as she did. The things you did at home did not apply in this unrelated landscape. There was no one to advise you. She found out that the beautiful buildings and shops in the heart of the city were occupied only by politicians and pilgrims. One day she looked out her window and the entire street was filled with foreigners, and a white man with no legs who was in a wheeled cart pulled along by a giant Alsatian dog. They were singing and cheering as if they had won a great victory and she stayed in her room all day, petrified. In the evening she crept down to the corner shop for something to eat and the Pakistani shopkeeper was giving out about the Notting Hill carnival.

She kept to herself and found work in a nice respectable coffee shop where each customer got their own pot of coffee and little pastries that were eaten with the side of a fork. The girls there were Spanish and Italian, and a Puerto Rican. They did not speak much English and spent their free time going to American films. Their lives were built around these excursions. They brought in bags of sandwiches and spoke gutturally in their own language throughout the performance, occasionally lifting their eyes to make admiring groans when Michelle Pfeiffer or Julia Roberts achieved a passionate understanding with some fellow strangely burnished beneath his clothes, as if he had been sanded and then waxed.

J never asked that of her. 'I have nothing to give you,' he said. 'I want nothing from you except to admire you.' He turned up his hands to show both their emptiness and that they concealed no tricks. She gazed with pleasure on the smoothness of his palms and his short, clean nails. At home, if a man said he didn't want a cup of tea, there was a moral obligation to brew up at once. When she pressed him to kiss her he refused before obliging her with a dry, shy kiss and then he smiled at her sadly and said, 'Oh, I must just have another,' and he began to consume her in small mouthfuls, before falling on her, like a dog on its dinner. She had been shocked by his eagerness, shocked by the whole thing, which gave her a sudden sharp understanding of her mother, but afterwards he was so grateful that she could only feel she had not given him enough. The awful thing was that although she had not enjoyed the event, it made her fall in love with him. Now instead of his umbrella, she carried around the whole baggage of

That Bad Woman

his life, the plays and poems and sides of beef. J had a phone installed so that she would not have to run down to the public phone in the hall which was adorned with notices from women offering to torture men in return for money. After that he rarely called. Sometimes she did not see him for weeks on end. She could not tell if it was him she missed or the life he lived without her. She was so obsessed with the thought of the things he did apart from her that she could not be happy when they were together. 'You must not sit around like a servant girl waiting for romance,' he rebuked her. She tried to explain that it wasn't just romance she craved, it was the life he had mentioned. He laughed and told her the things he described did not belong to him, she could avail herself of them any time she wished. He made out a list of places for her to visit, but the galleries and concert halls were full of sour Americans, disguised in expensive English raincoats, and she thought that culture was a cold thing when you could not laugh with someone at the pictures of naked men and women or touch their hand when the music was soulful. Once he mentioned a club he belonged to, a gentlemen's club. 'It's rather grand,' he said in that way he had, as if apologising.

'Take me there,' she said.

'You'd be bored,' he smiled. But he had spoken of his club with reverence and in her mind it became the equivalent of paradise.

When she was not waiting for the telephone she spent

most of her time in a park, walking and sometimes talking to other foreigners who sat on benches. It was to one of these she confided that she was pregnant. 'Go home,' he said, not to dismiss her, but to use his small store of English words usefully. She longed for home but she could not go back even though when the baby arrived everyone would dote on it. She remembered the merriment of the younger women, the careless slide into domesticity and how sometimes when they had had eight or nine kids they would shake themselves off and go to university or enter politics. The women always ridiculed sex, removing the sting with a swipe of sarcasm. She missed their softness that was like the softness of rain, and the knife edge of their humour. She missed them so much it was like a sickness. And then – lunatic – she found herself nostalgic for the men, whose irresponsible ways meant you never had to take them seriously. She stayed in the flat for a week counting whorls and dots on the virulent old wallpaper and then she just stayed there because the coffee shop seemed too decorous a place for her now. She began to look forward to having a child. As soon as the notion of it became a reality she felt stronger. She made up her mind to go and look for J, although she had no idea where to find him. Then she remembered his club and looked it up in the phone book. It amazed her to think she could have gone there at any time but had only got the courage because she was at the end of her tether.

That Bad Woman

A flunkey took her coat at the door. 'Who are you meeting?'

'J,' she said boldly, because she didn't actually know his name.

Like magic he directed her up the stairs and told her to turn left for the visitors' lounge. And it was kind of like a fairy tale, the big curving staircase and the ceiling dripping with chandeliers. She ventured into a room full of men in suits and roosted on a hard leather sofa. While she waited, a galdy oul' lad with his eye on her bust asked her would she care for a spot of bubbly. She was looking around her all the time to see would J come in and her new friend urged her to relax. But she couldn't. She didn't fit in. She could tell from the look of the club members that dowdiness was *de rigueur*. People were staring at her dress. The champagne arrived but they hadn't the proper glasses and put big silver tankards on the table.

'Are they pure silver?' she asked.

'Not exactly,' the old lad said in his buttered shortbread voice. Not *exactly*. Tin more like. And then she had to jump up and tell him she needed the toilet.

Ah, now, that was beautiful. She had an urge to write home to her mother about that toilet. The long mirrors were like looking into a lake. There were flowers and little bottles of water, like Lourdes water only they were for drinking, and ladies who dabbed their noses in a very discreet way, as if it was an act akin to wiping your bottom. The women had a vegetable look, like something grown underwater or nurtured in a walled garden. There wasn't a mark on them. Their bland bosoms had been sketched in by some artist with averted eye. She went into a cubicle to check and, sure enough, her aunt had arrived. Already there was a mark showing on her brocade skirt. She patched herself up with toilet paper and poked out her head. 'Has anybody here got a sanitary towel – the loan of a sanitary towel – please?' The women said nothing although one of them smiled at her. Possibly they had a different arrangement down there, or had found some long-term method of coping with it. 'Thank you anyway,' she said. She could feel them watching the small scarlet stain shaped like a star when she left. Probably they would think she had been shot in the arse. She couldn't go back into the big room for she felt certain that whatever the ladies might think, the men would know. She was sorry about her gentleman, left alone in all that stuffy grandeur to drink champagne out of tin mugs.

She walked around the city for hours, not caring that she was bleeding, bumping into tourists who were looking for strange women to sleep with, and lonely foreigners with zombie eyes. When the night had consumed all its leftover souls she stood alone in some big gaunt place that was marked by a monumental arch. She leaned against the arch to rest and there, beneath it, was a little bundle rolled up in a pink blanket. 'Oh, a baby!' she cried. Someone had left a baby. As she pulled back the blanket she thanked Saint Anthony for finding a replacement for her own little

That Bad Woman

lost baby. A girl, barely teenage, reared up her head. She was rickety thin, her face as grey as nuns' porridge. Kathleen gazed, first in amazement and then in pity. 'Oh, you creature!' she said.

The girl eyed her sleepily. 'Got any money?'

'What you need is nourishment,' Kathleen said firmly. 'You need a proper place to sleep.'

The girl told her to fuck herself. Her little sparrow's wrist struck out and while Kathleen was nursing her face the girl snatched her handbag and vanished like a skinny demon into the dark.

Once, on the underground, she heard this announcement: 'If passenger Pavelzciek is on this train, would he please proceed to Trafalgar Square, where his mother is waiting.' Everyone laughed except Kathleen who closed her eyes and felt with Pavelzciek's mother the panic of recognising no one, of being left alone with the guzzling pigeons, afraid to move from this seething spot in case you never again laid eyes on the only thing you knew.

The most shaming thing was that he wasn't even married. A few weeks afterwards she spotted him getting into a taxi and she followed in another taxi. She knocked on the door of a house in Marylebone that bore his name beneath a bell and barged in past him, into his flat, and without a word she had poked into everything, into his fridge with its little tinfoil ashtrays of frozen meals for one. 'You haven't even got a wife,' she accused him.

He defended himself, holding up his empty palms in

that way he had. 'I never said I was married.' He was watching her with an odd sort of gravity and it took her a minute to realise that she had hurt his feelings. 'I'm very fond of you,' he said. 'Don't think I have been hiding anything from you. Quite the opposite. I have been sparing you. You and I have shared a remarkable happiness in spite of our differences but as far as my life is concerned, darling girl, you would be bored and unhappy.'

She tried to make sense of this but she was confused. She had imagined his flat would be very grand but it was shabby, not with the respectable dowdiness of his club but in a lonely way, as if life was dwindling around him. Kathleen thought that even though she had made it out of the sticks and got herself a man with a very high up job in the government, the subtleties always eluded her and possibly she wasn't really very bright.

She ate a little bit of the red cabbage from her salad and some brown bread and butter. The rain had stopped and black taxis, shiny as eels, hissed on the wet road. A weak sun put a halo of mist on rooftops and a faint tinge in the sky, a delicate lemon yellow like ladies' pee. She walked back, thinking of a dog she once had, a wall-eyed creature called Scrap, which had no idea of its function as sheepdog and stole a lamb and smuggled it into its bed and nurtured it after its pups had been drowned. She bought a bunch of anemones, thinking they would catch the last rays of sun through her window and draw the eye away from the wicked little sink with its pipes exposed, like a spiteful

That Bad Woman

beggar showing off his deformities, but the sun had gone down and the Jamaicans had begun to fight and she had set herself the task of counting stars as they took their places in the sky by the time she heard the doorbell's peevish drone. 'Terrible day.' He kissed her cheek. 'You don't know how I envy you your simple life.' He kissed her lips in a fatherly way and she began to relax. There wasn't anything devouring in his kisses. They weren't even exciting. They made her sleepy. When she was in his arms she couldn't imagine why she suffered so much when they were apart. He lowered her onto the bed and his jacket grazed her face. It smelled of wool and had a hard edge like a rope. His legs grew restless and he grasped and pulled at her as if he was trying to get his footing on a cliff face. Something about her – not her personality, she knew – had tripped a switch, and he was off on his demented quest like a prisoner trying to dig a tunnel with a teaspoon.

To make the time pass she thought about a Russian she had met in the park. He was beautifully dressed but had the look of a refugee. His sad face gave her permission to sit down beside him, and to break the ice she asked him why he had come to London. It was the phrase 'Thatcher's Britain', he said. It made him think of a pleasant place with thatched houses and fields of hay and employment for all. She asked him if he liked the city. He said nothing but stared ahead and she thought that behind that gaze, both blank and intent, he still saw a sun-warmed scene of honest labour and contentment. 'What do you like best?' she persisted. When he told her the rats' kitchen, she thought it was a joke – some dosshouse he was staying at – but she could see he hadn't a sense of humour. Actually, it was interesting. It was an attraction they had at Regent's Park zoo, a cage that had been equipped with chairs and tables and utensils and every manner of home comfort to see how the rats would adapt to domestic life, and they lived like lords, in and out of their kitchen, holding little tea parties. 'It is proof,' said the Russian, 'that any creature, given a chance, will improve itself.'

One of these days she would go to Regent's Park to see for herself the rats' kitchen but in the meantime she got pleasure from taking out the notion of it now and then and turning it over, the finicky little creatures entering this minefield of a cage, full of obstacles and breakables. She pictured them puzzling over the cups with their dainty little claws, gnawing at the legs of chairs to get the feel of them. Had someone given them an inkling, a bit of training, perhaps, in the correct use of knives and forks, or had they to bash along like everyone else? She saw them seated around the kitchen table sipping their cups of tea, arresting the crumbs of cake on their plate with tiny little silver forks, perhaps making small talk in rat language and scarcely able to believe their luck.

Life on Mars

Midway through dying, Tom grew unfaithful to Anna. He accepted her necessary ministrations with cold politeness, his impatient eye resenting the time until he could go back to his new mistress, his pain. He had no word for her when he went. She couldn't recognise the gaunt figure on the pillow. She could not even call him love. All she could think was that whoever he was, he had been hers and now she had nothing.

A little while after his death he came back to her. She had got into the habit of saying his name as she walked in the door just to hear some familiar sound. One day there was a response – not a voice or anything like that. She came into the house and found that he was there. The diplomacy of privacy, which is agreed in every marriage, was gone. He was there as he had never been, except in part or at odd moments. His closeness made her weak, almost complacent. She did not bother to dress or eat or

That Bad Woman

make any contact with the world outside. People tried to prise her from her mourning and she put down the phone on them or shut the door. There wasn't any room for them.

While she was sleeping he went away. She woke to find the house empty. 'Tom?' she whispered. 'Oh, Tom, *please.*' She couldn't forgive him. He had not, after all, been taken away from her by death. That was just a poor sick body where he had been held as prisoner. He had come back in all his strength to break her to his will and then he had left her. She could not even think of him now. She took down his photographs and put them away.

She found widowhood to be an exclusive and alien colony. Nobody liked her much the way she was. Friends wanted to take her out of herself. Where on earth did they think she would go, dragged forth from her last hiding place?

Just as individuals frequently decide to fall in love or to fall ill as their needs demand, there is a moment when people decide to go mad, and as Anna didn't want anybody or anything else, she thought that madness would do quite nicely. She developed a strange, swift gait, like a woman who knows she is being followed. At home, and even in the street, she talked to herself. *You're mad, you know that*, she reproached herself, but without dismay. She felt quite successful when she started to see flying saucers.

She had come into the kitchen to make herself some tea

Life on Mars

but instead she poured a glass of gin. She drank it standing at the sink, looking out the window over the garden wall at a sunset which seemed to cling around a naked apple tree like a bright scarf. In the distance, where it was still blue, her vision was spotted by a little cell cluster. She blinked to get rid of this distortion and the dots parted and began to sail towards her. She watched intently until they were no longer dots but discs, shimmering and transparent. When they got to tea plate size she could see that they were not flat but perhaps lenticular, and that they had legs or tripods or some sort of landing device. As they passed over the horizon, violent colours exploded off their surface from the burning sun. When the larger planet subsided and the sky grew dark they could no longer be seen although they must still be there, if they had ever been there. 'UFOs!' She spoke to herself, as had become habitual. 'Unidentifieds fuck off!' She rinsed her glass with the economical housekeeping of the solo dweller and gave her mad laugh. 'Lucky me, I suppose, that I've got no one to tell.'

They were there again the following day. She hadn't even had any gin. She watched until the dots turned into discs and screwed up her eyes when they passed the sun so that she could see them as they drifted into dusk. It seemed now that the rims of the saucers had no actual substance but were a shimmering aura surrounding some central body. There was definitely an extension, legs or antennae or something.

After a few days she found that she was waiting for

That Bad Woman

them. At a certain time in the day she interrupted whatever pointless thing she was doing and moved to her post by the sink. As the sun ripened and cooled, the weighty dullness shifted a fraction in her chest. She never particularly wondered who they were or what they wanted but they made her think of a line from an old movie: 'We are not alone.' She was glad of that. When it got dark she thought she could still see them, skimming and hovering playfully around one another in the dusty purple shadows, but maybe she just imagined she did.

One day they landed in her garden. She stood in utter silence, feeling the shimmer of their approach and then a soft 'whoosh' as they touched down in the grass. She was almost glad there was no one in the house. She had learnt how to hold herself still, how to breathe without disturbing the air. When she finally went to investigate she laughed out loud. There were only four children in the garden. They must have climbed over the wall to get at the few knobs of blighted apples that still clung to her tree.

'What are you doing here?' She attempted severity.

The children looked at one another. 'We're not really doing anything, if that's all right.' They disentangled themselves and stood up, shaking out their wings. In the light from the kitchen window she could see them clearly. The shimmering discs were not saucers but an atmosphere, a thick aureole of light that surrounded them.

'Who are you?' she breathed.

Life on Mars

'You are a who,' they corrected. 'We are not a who.'

'Fairies?' she said. 'Or are you angels? I've been watching you from a distance. I thought you were those funny things that crazy people see – unidentified flying objects.'

They nodded and seemed pleased with this, although their expression did not change. They had no expression. Whatever they were, they were reliable. She could count off the seconds on her watch until they made their landing in the grass each night and then, for some measureless time, she was distracted from her loneliness. Mostly, she talked about Tom. They were only children but their solemn faces made them good listeners. They never spoke about themselves. She came to realise that this was because they had no ego, but when she questioned them they answered politely.

'Where are you from?'

'We come from Mars.'

'But there is no life on Mars!'

'Where there is no other life,' they told her, 'that is where we are.'

'How can I see you when no one else can?' She followed them as they ventured into the house, inspecting things as children do.

'Anyone can see us,' they shrugged. 'People don't look. Hardly anyone looks at the world. They only see what's in their own life.'

'Except where there is no life . . .' she mused, and they nodded earnestly.

That Bad Woman

It explained, anyway, why it was always weirdos who saw flying saucers, but she wondered why they told other people. She never wanted to. She wanted to keep them to herself, and she wanted to please them. She wanted to give them a treat, like ordinary children. 'Is there anything you like?' she asked them.

'Yes!' they said. 'Everything.'

'Have whatever you want,' she said. 'Choose something.'

They explored her kitchen earnestly, each selecting a treasure – a china cup printed with blue flowers, a photograph of Anna as a child, a magnifying glass.

'That's just a glass, there's nothing special about that,' Anna said.

'It was special the day it was invented,' the child said. 'We do not know time as a dimension. Because we are no age and every age, all things are both old and new.'

'What beautiful creatures you are,' Anna marvelled. 'Are there any creatures in the universe more beautiful than you?'

'Grasshoppers!' they cried. 'Water beetles!'

One day she saw Tom again. It was nine months after his death and she had gone into the city to hear a reading by a novelist. While she was there she ran into a woman she knew and they decided to stay in town for supper. They talked about the writer's last novel, her awful clothes, her predilection for younger men. They drank a nice bottle of wine. Anna was enjoying herself. For the first time since Tom's death she was aware of other people. She turned to look at the rest of the diners and her eye hovered on a handsome man who looked a bit familiar. For a moment he looked like Tom. Something about his chin reminded her of Tom's chin and while she pondered this the man's face turned into Tom's face. *I want to touch his face*, she thought. *I can't bear this*. She glanced again but the man had turned back into himself, back into someone else's man. She waited for the agony to loosen its grip. It wouldn't let go. *Maybe if I could get home and cry,* she thought. She got away from the restaurant and into her car. All the way home the pain tore at her like something that urgently needed to be delivered. She stumbled into the house, putting on the heat, pouring a drink so that everything would be in readiness for her grief. Nothing came. She crouched on the floor, drinking, absently aware of an ache that had settled into her and was violent and impersonal. It did not even evoke Tom. It had turned into some stranger who ground his boot into her chest until she submitted and accepted its imprint of ridges and studs. It went on for weeks, fading into something dull and dirty. Tom was nowhere to be found. First he had gone and then his love had gone. He was wedded now, to something else. It wasn't polite, any more, to hanker.

She looked at her reflection. *I am turning into another person*, she thought. *When I married Tom I agreed to leave behind the girl I was, to be whatever he wanted. After he died I was waiting to go back, but that was impossible because then the only logical thing would be to start all over again.* She had always done what her husband wanted, not out of weakness but because of a sense of rightness. There wasn't any threat of distortion, only the promise of ripening. Now it was time to let go. In her mind she agreed to this, but the spirit is more accepting than the flesh. Her metabolism rebelled, shot grey through her hair, pulled down the edges of her mouth, put a warning look in her eye. The things she used to apply to make herself pretty – the juicy glints for lip and cheek, the alluring eye tints – sat on her bleak face like rocks of quartz in a desert. She would not give in. She put on what Tom used to call bonking music and hurled herself around to keep her figure in shape but she only achieved the thinness of a beaten dog. After a prolonged hostility she decided to make friends with the monster in the mirror. 'Hello, hag,' she said. The beast grinned back eagerly.

That evening as she was washing her dish she looked up and saw spots around the sun. 'Oh,' she said, and tears of longing filled her eyes.

'I've missed you so much,' she told them. 'Why didn't you come?'

'We were there!' They sounded exactly like ordinary children, high-pitched and self-righteous. 'You didn't look for us.'

For the first time they allowed her to touch them. They had a substance, their cheeks, the hollows of their shoulders. They had a texture, they were completely real. *They trust me*, she thought. *They are as soft as nothing and yet they trust me.* She felt them smile, although they could not smile. They leaned into her. One by one they slept. When she woke they were gone but she had rested without the glare of greyness behind her eyes.

As she waited for their next visit something of tremendous importance occurred to her. She could not wait to question them and the minute they appeared she demanded to know. 'If your time is without dimension, then what about my husband? In another time he was alive. Is he now in some other dimension?'

They watched her guardedly. 'This is your dimension.'

'He was my husband,' she said angrily. They flinched from her but she couldn't help it. She felt certain they knew. 'You don't understand what it's like to love someone and then lose them and never know where they went. I have to know. It's important.'

'It's not important.' They moved away from her. They crouched down in the night-frosted grass and began to pick daisies. 'It's none of your business.'

'That's so cruel!' Anna said.

'We cannot be cruel.' They looked up at her blankly. 'We can't be kind. We do not have imagination.'

She slammed back into the house. She could sense the shock vibrating in their wings and her own resentment coarsely beating in her chest. For a long time she felt them waiting for her in the dark and then the night

That Bad Woman

emptied and there were only tomcats and owls and ordinary things out there.

In the morning she phoned a hairdresser and had the grey taken out of her hair. She bought a bag of clothes and had lunch in a wine bar and then, slightly tipsy, went into a travel agent and ordered up a week in the sun. In Barcelona she met a nice man called Sam Maguire. He made her interested in food again and they talked. She told him about Tom but she did not say anything about her visitors. They were nothing to do with him. Tom was her link with this world and they connected her to another world.

'You've had a hard time,' Sam Maguire said kindly.

'I've had a good life,' she said, surprising herself. Nothing else happened but she was pleased that he asked for her telephone number.

When she got home she was taken aback by the abandoned look of the place. She cleaned it vigorously, enjoying the vacuum cleaner's appetite, the astringent reek of bleach. Then she went to the shops and bought food and flowers. The house looked fresh and clean but it looked like someone else's house. She retrieved Tom's photographs and put them around the rooms. After that she went to bed and slept until noon.

The following evening she took up her place at the window. The sun went down and stars climbed into a muted sky. She began to be afraid. 'I'm here,' she whispered. 'Can't you see me? I know you're there.' Inside her

Life on Mars

house the phone began to ring. *Sam*, she thought. She let it ring a long time but she wanted to hear his voice so she went to answer it, switching on the light so that the sky outside became an inky plate crumbed with unknown worlds.

Gods and Slaves

Their mother always said that if any of the girls got pregnant their father would throw her out in the street. This warning acted more effectively than any threat to their own security, keeping them in a state of grace for longer than was necessary or appealing. Modesty flowed around them like a moat and there was no brother who might act as drawbridge. They wondered about men a great deal and sometimes begged their mother, 'What is a man like?' and she replied that if they wanted to know what men were like they had only to look at the picture in the hall. The picture was a framed photograph of Roman statuary, gods or slaves, but the chiselled unmentionables had crumbled into dust long before the camera was invented and they had to ply their fervid imaginations to vague porous whorls, not very large, they suspected, even before air pollution had attacked their finer points.

That Bad Woman

It is likely that they would have continued gazing vexedly at this faded image until middle age dimmed their eyesight had not Phelim Hartigan appeared. From that moment it became clear that at least one female in the household was going to be seduced and each one was alert to the event. The mother wore high heels and hid her hair net. The girls washed their long blonde hair in camomile flowers and did special exercises that promised bosoms as big as melons. Phelim Hartigan was not a tall man but was of a forceful structure. Other men looked like suits filled with cushions or coat hangers, but he was all muscle, sprung from a root of generation. He had thick black curly hair and green eyes and when he sang in *basso profundo* it sent vibrations right up through the furniture and through the person who was sitting on it too. From the moment he entered the house his prerogative was established. The black cat, Mrs Danvers, flung herself on his knee and picked impatiently at the weave of his trousers. Even the father, when he opened the door, appeared to be handing him a menu.

They got Phelim through an advertisement. The sisters sang in close harmony in the manner of the Andrews Sisters for the entertainment or endurance of visitors at Christmas. As they came into their teens the notion presented itself that this talent might transport them into the larger world, where men were. Their mother was very proud of them and relaxed her normal

Gods and Slaves

vigilance to see their gifts admired. They were paid ten shillings a week to sing in variety concerts for which she sewed up an assortment of costumes, depending on her mood. Sometimes they were chaste white frocks in cotton piqué and on other occasions they were scarlet satin shifts through which the unfulfilled peaks of their whirlpool bras pointed like the horns of minor pantomime devils.

The theatres were in the poor suburbs of Dublin and had been first cinemas and then bingo halls. Cinerama was dragooned in as a final bid to save the cinemas. Trains apparently came off their rails and hurtled into the audience or rivers were seen to burst their banks and explode through the screen. Stereophonic systems surrounded the audience with noises of disaster, but neither miracles nor disaster can compensate a loss of faith. With the start of the sixties people had jobs and money. They wanted real life. This fad was short-lived. Later on the picture houses would be pool halls or carpet warehouses but for a few years variety became popular, with clamorous rock groups imitating the Crickets or the Comets and male comedians who dressed as women, stuffing cabbages inside their jumpers.

The girls stood rigid upon the stage, one day perky as the models in Persil ads, the next sleekly gleaming like women in motor oil commercials. They made uniform swipes at the air with their hands, and their voices, tonally perfect, flowed about them like a cloud of summer flies.

That Bad Woman

But they got no further. People in the nearest rows looked bewildered. 'We can't hear you.' When they moved close to the microphone it whistled. 'Get them off ya!' yelled the gurriers from the back. Within a few weeks everyone got used to the silent girl performers, as they had once accepted silent films, and they continued to appear weekly, but neither their careers nor their lives progressed. In the dressing area, with the smell of cold sweat and beer, they were timidly pawed by midget pop performers. A squint-eyed comedian in his forties invited Kay, who was thirteen, to dinner. She asked could her sisters come too and he, gazing soulfully askew, declared, 'There are times when a man likes to be alone with a woman.' They decided that they must look for more sophisticated outlets, nightclubs or television. They auditioned for television, where the volume could be adjusted with knobs, but were turned down on the basis that they were lacking in 'oomph'.

For two shillings you could place a card in the window of a music shop on the quays and it was like purchasing a magic spell. 'All-girl professional singing group seeks male backing,' the notice read. A stream of young men arrived at the house, where once it had seemed that no man would ever come. They travelled on foot, by bicycle, on throbbing motorbikes, with guitars, mouth organs, accordions. Most of them were wan and spotty, no adepts in oomph. The sisters had lived too long on a diet of pure romance to accommodate any imperfection.

Gods and Slaves

They entertained a good-looking country boy until a dispute arose about the division of their fee. 'What do ye care about cash?' he had said bitterly. 'Youse birds are sittin' on a fortune.' After a series of disappointments they took to stationing themselves within the folds of the drawing room curtains, and there they lived, quiet as the cat. When a fresh applicant pushed the creaky gate they would signal one another and make a swift appraisal before informing the youth that the position had been filled.

The notice in the music shop must have grown sallow and flyblown by the time Phelim Hartigan found it, for several years had passed and the girls had all but given up singing for more useful pursuits, such as typing and dressmaking. Kay came home from school one day and found him sitting in the dining room strumming his guitar and singing in his beautiful deep voice. He fixed his eye on her and sang on, and she grew very pale and then very red, and fled to the kitchen. Mother was thrashing pastry with a rolling pin. 'That is Mr Hartigan. He is to accompany you girls,' she said and then, surprising her youngest daughter beyond all measure, 'I have invited him to tea.'

They never knew where Phelim came from. He was much older than the other young men, being about twenty-nine. They had no idea why he answered the advertisement, for he was a good musician as well as a good singer. They questioned him but he rarely made

That Bad Woman

conversation. He would strum a few pulsating chords and name a song. He began in a voice that was low and sweet but carried strongly and they, without any direction, followed in, as a woman is led by a skilled dance partner. Their voices, which had been bland and thin, at once improved, for the exciting male presence injected their singing with a tremolo of yearning. They knew every time they opened their mouths that life had begun. That fundamental tremor was akin to a biblical upheaval that could breathe life into dust, roll back the stones from caves, rend their clothing, make them free to do anything. Yet they had been brought up as spinsters. They had no idea how to persuade. 'Rehearsals twice a week,' they told Phelim sharply. (They had always been once a week.) On the days between they silently examined their noses for blackheads and blew on their palms to test their breath.

'Stand up straight,' he commanded Maeve. 'Of the four of us, you are the only one with breasts. Little breasts, but let them be seen.' The girls eyed him suspiciously. No one said breasts. Bosoms were all right, being a joke word, but breasts were a portion of the anatomy not openly acknowledged between the sexes. 'Let down your hair,' he told Cecilia. He unpinned her plaits and raked them loose with his fingers. An electrified cornfield fled over her shoulders. 'You girls cannot hold your breath for the whole of your lives.' He inhaled deeply, allowing the air to go all the way down his body. 'You must sing from . . .

Gods and Slaves

here.' And before their very eyes he touched himself. There. They had stopped breathing completely, their eyes riveted to that part of his clothing that had a restless, lumpy look, like a boy's pocket where a mouse was hidden.

Two weeks later the restructured group made its first appearance at the Apollo in Sundrive. The girls had begun to change. Released from the petrifying spell of innocence, they were less gawky, less astonished. Touches of colour appeared in their cheeks. They no longer carried their bodies as the mortifying baggage of looming fecundity, but with a swish, like the net slips, stiffened with sugar, they introduced beneath their skirts accentuated with Waspee belts. Toenails, hitherto the yellow torment of an older generation (hewn into a V when ingrown), became pearly lozenges, winking through peep-toe shoes. The sisters were in white. He wore black – black shirt, black leather jacket and jeans. The audience looked rebellious. They remembered the silent girl trio fondly. Phelim began to mumble something unrecognisable in a little Woody Guthrie voice, making the audience strain to listen. When they were lulled he made a mighty twang on his guitar, gyrated the middle portion of his anatomy and the song became recognisable as 'Jailhouse Rock'. The girls clapped their hands and bent into the microphone for the chorus. Phelim thrust his guitar floorward as if to tango, bent backwards with angled knees, projected his hips at unsuspecting housewives and filled

That Bad Woman

the cold little theatre with his great warm voice. The women in the audience did something that no Dublin audience had ever done before. They screamed. That night their weekly earnings were promoted to thirty shillings a week.

For a moment, poised before the baying housewives, the sisters had felt afraid. Then melodic whistles interposed the soughing dirge and this was pulsed with the crisp percussion of applause. Phelim was laughing as he gathered them forward to share the praise. The wall of discord that swept around them like Cinerama became a jubilee march. The scuffed stage was a triumphal platform. Acid stage lights on twisted wires rained down dazzling splinters that dusted their hair and their white dresses with gold. Oh, they understood they were not fit for worship, they were ordinary women who knew better than to rise above their station, but they were the brides of an idol. Phelim their creature. The sisters exchanged sated glances. They felt fulfilled, accomplished. They had achieved the primary object of mating, which is to make other women jealous.

The idyll that followed this conquest was of short duration. The notion crept in on them that each of the sisters was another woman. A man could not be jointly claimed. Possession was a singular objective. The enchantment of his appearance in their life was soured by the need to clarify his position in it. All their lives they had been fused by curiosity. Now they were sundered by the more

Gods and Slaves

powerful force of rivalry. When Phelim gave Cecilia a lift on the pillion of his motorcycle, Maeve stormed out of the house and came back with a startled boy, whom she called a boyfriend. Kay wore a dress so short that her mother said she would be ashamed to have it hanging on her clothesline, let alone on her daughter.

The brides were stymied. All their efforts to claim his attention appeared only to cultivate his indifference. One day he did not appear for rehearsal. 'And I had bought crinkle chips for tea,' the mother said disconsolately. It was not to be a solo occurrence. He told the girls he had other things on his mind, there was a difficult decision he had to make. Delight deserted them. They grew anxious, inert, waiting for him to make the difficult choice between them. 'Of course,' the mother crushingly mused, 'a man like that would have other women.' Had they not been so uncomfortably tethered by the baffling hex they might have taken pleasure in the success of their singing. The group had been offered a fee of three pounds by a rival theatre. They were invited once again to audition for television.

All week the mother laboured on their new costumes, cream art silk with gold coin spots. All day they steamed their skin, singed their hair and scraped tiny golden strands from their legs, tautly humming choruses and harmonies. They had been stiffly poised in the drawing room for half an hour awaiting Phelim when the doorbell rang. Their mother went to answer it so that their attention had fled

That Bad Woman

with her to the hall even as they listened to the news on the wireless that President John Kennedy had been assassinated. The mother came back and leaned in the doorway. She seemed shaken, as if she had received the same terrible bulletin at the door. 'That was a boy,' she said. 'He was sent by Phelim. Phelim will not be coming. He will not be coming back at all.'

The girls sang alone at the audition. They were turned down, as they knew they would be. When this was out of the way they found themselves husbands as quickly as possible. Even Kay, shrugging off her school bag, broke her mother's heart by riling a boy with her short skirt and struggling up the aisle as a teenage bride and mother-to-be.

They talked about Phelim only once after his disappearance.

'He is dead,' Maeve decided. 'Mother would not tell us.'

'An accident with his motorbike,' Cecilia agreed.

And Kay proposed that if not dead, then he had certainly been called to the priesthood. Any other possibilities were too painful to contemplate, but even this resolution brought no relief. It only turned them into women. That the Lord should claim two such prizes on a single day! After all, there was no contest, only sport for the gods.

They settled down to marriage with that look of bewilderment and resignation that young wives had before the

Gods and Slaves

Beatles. They never again regained the closeness of their childhood for they had been healed of curiosity and naturally, they no longer had recourse to the question, 'What is a man like?'

The Secret Diary of Mrs Rochester

There was no possibility of taking a walk that day. The sky was flooded grey and the wind was aroused to a malignant frenzy. Fainting branches clawed at my window and birds held their breath as the forest giants wrestled with invisible foe. Yet it was not the storm that hampered me. I was at the mercy of an element less rational than tempest.

A year ago, I had returned to Thornfield Hall, an heiress, an independent woman with a set of new cousins to my credit, and from one of these a proposal of marriage which I had to decline for its want of warmth. I found my master as reduced as I was advantaged – one eye gone and the other destroyed, missing an arm, burnt out of his manor house and widowed by the most tragical circumstance. At first my pity warred with anger to see a proud giant stumble like a fledgling raw to flight. But compassion was the greater since I too had once been helpless and dependent. This, then, was God's leavening – to catch

That Bad Woman

the falling sparrow; to lay the lion down with the lamb. Reader, I married him.

It is not commonplace to give an unrelieved account of married life so I have set down what is agreeable and reserve the factual report for my private diary, in the hope that it may one day find that true reader who requires not to be assured that all ended happily, but remains curious to learn the point of resolution between human aspiration and human nature.

I will not pretend that ours was an ordinary marriage for of necessity it reached into the realm of the fantastic. I was compelled to be my master's eyes but my vision of life is a plain one whereas his divination dwelt within his head and was whatever capricious fancy served up to him. On woodlands walks I strove to illuminate his dark path by describing the trail which Providence had laid in that sombre place as intimations of Paradise, a posy of wild flowers, a dainty tracery of ferns, a family of fair-skinned mushrooms. But my master prefers a beauty of the man-made kind and would disturb my narration with a kiss. 'There is but one enchantment in this forest. My Jane. My provoking beauty. My little angel.'

What did he see then? 'No beauty,' I reminded him. 'Nor angel as I live. I am as I have always been – puny and insignificant.'

'Ah, Jane – if you could see yourself as I see you.'

I touched his wounded lion's face. 'Oh, Edward. If you could only see again.'

The Secret Diary of Mrs Rochester

Yet vision is more than the eye can see, agility more than ably directed limbs. We knew the swiftness of sympathy and our days were radiant with affection's transforming light. At times I prided myself that I could be better eyes than those brooding torches that had once lit his world, for my gaze was not clouded by past regret nor my joy in beholding compromised by dissipation. I ought to have been wary of exultation for experience has taught me that pride may precipitate a calamitous descent. We had been married six months when two small incidents set in motion a leviathan of change. The first was a letter from my cousin St John Rivers. It was touching in its plainness and showed a new humility born of the breadth of stern experience. I was relieved that he had forgiven my rejection. I wrote back and found a curious balm in plain speaking, without any need to adorn. I told him of the practicalities of my married life but not of its peculiarities, and especially not of a remarkable proposal that I had just received from Mr Rochester which was to mark the second change. He declared that we were to commence the travels planned for our honeymoon in that ghastly time when he still had a poor fiend of a wife hidden in the house. 'You shall sojourn at Paris, Rome and Vienna,' he avowed anew. 'All the ground I have wandered over shall be retrodden by you: where I stamped my foot, your sylph's foot shall step also.'

What had once been esteemed a grand plan was now mere parody. To think of that same proudly stamping foot

That Bad Woman

stumbling on crowded foreign pavements was beyond pity. I at once declined and declared that I was too well occupied for such frivolity. When he saw that I was in earnest he was sullen a day or two but then resorted to cajolery. 'Ah, Miss Pinprick! I am restless and discouraged. If you will not let me feel the sun upon my blind brow, indulge me with a ramble in my rambling mind. Let me share with you the travels I have already enjoyed.'

To this I consented. We became fireside travellers. In picturesque memory he was my guide through majestic mountain passes, along fashionable promenades. I began to look forward to our nightly adventures, though I deemed them best consigned to history and narrative for their self-indulgent nature. Once or twice he strayed into places I should not suffer my foot to trespass even in fancy and I smartly rebuked him. I had anticipated that as a husband he might grow difficult to please but was unprepared for a conflict that struck not merely at the heart of our union but at its very soul. I yearned to be joined with him upon a path to virtue and he required my presence at those worldly sites that had most profoundly jolted his sensibilities. Perhaps because of his ruined sight his will was stronger than mine, for ere long I had trepidation for company on each of our journeys, and regret for supper in some bawdy inn at which we sojourned. I urged him to restrain his chronicle to nature's attributes but we must have exhausted all of Europe's scenery, for one night (when I was ill attired for

The Secret Diary of Mrs Rochester

it and had a piece of sewing in my hand) he goaded me into society. 'Did I ever tell you,' said he, 'about my first meeting with Céline Varens?'

I was so provoked my needlework fell to the ground. 'Must I remind you that lady set you on the path to ruin?'

He bent to retrieve my sewing and, in restoring it to me, rested a weary hand upon my knee. 'If that was ruin, then what am I come to now?'

'Acceptance, I hope – and virtue – an element not foremost in the female society enjoyed on your travels.' I kept my voice calm but could feel my heart challenge the sturdy seams of my grey house dress.

'You are right, Jane, they were not virtuous.' He uttered a sigh such as might issue from a captive lion, from the depths of his thwarted animal nature, and then fell to a silence that neither teasing nor intellectual discourse could repair. Then in a voice barely discernible he murmured, 'Ah, but they were beautiful.' There was another void which I was helpless to repair until at last, in a tone of grievous wistfulness, he enquired, 'How are you attired?'

I often had told him that I could be nothing other than I was. Yet something warned me that this need for feminine appeasement was a wound that must be stanched. I took a deep breath and begged heaven's understanding. 'It is a muslin tea gown, sir, with puffs and rosettes. I made it myself.' By this he seemed genuinely assuaged. 'Beguiling elf! So you are as other women after all.'

Yet it was hard to be the eyes of another, and more still

That Bad Woman

of a man, for they do not see as women see, and sometimes, for all my efforts to please, I caught his old scowling look and felt he wished to be alone to do some manly valeting on his head. A part of the difficulty lay in our location. Densely wrapped in forest, Ferndean was not a cheerful place. Edward had once declared that he could not put his mad wife there for fear its climate would end her wretched life. If he could see I felt sure he would have released us from the forest's clammy hold. Sunlight never entered our house and our garden supported no growth save weeping lichens. At times I felt their ranks o'ergrew my very self for, so far from the bedizened beauty I had invented of myself, I had grown paler and was prey to a persistent cough. I often thought of St John in India, and the fact that he too was struggling against an inclement climate. At such times a longing for his plain sincerity made me sit down and unburden myself to him in candid letters.

It was a foul winter. Indoors we lived at a high pitch of coquetry which both flattered and disquieted me (for I believe all deception to be folly). My husband was chivalrous but rarely serious and I accepted this as a necessary antidote to his sightless world but my own spirits were lowered by a communication from St John, who informed me without the least self-pity that his health was failing. In great humility he wondered if we had each committed an error of pride in undertaking a mission that might be beyond our courage to execute.

When the weather improved I led Mr Rochester for a

walk in the woods. His mood was gallant as we entered our familiar charade. 'What are you wearing, Jane?' I indulged him with description of some fashionable frippery. 'What, with brown leather boots?' he laughed. 'I have to say it, Jane, you have no taste in these matters.'

I was stung by his teasing, but far more by his perception. 'How do you know what I am wearing on my feet?'

He turned on me a most devilish look of amusement. 'Why, because it is quite enough for you to spend your evenings stitching away at complicated gowns without having to turn cobbler for my sightless admiration. We have not left Ferndean since we got married. You had no opportunity to buy new shoes.'

'How could you know what I was wearing when I came to Ferndean?' said I. 'You had not seen me for fully a year.'

Something about the wry manner in which he regarded me informed me so shockingly that I was almost robbed of one faculty just as he, apparently, had another restored. When I could speak again I uttered but a single phrase: 'You can see!'

'It's true, Jane.' He caught me up in his arms. 'I wanted to surprise you. I have regained a little sight.'

'When?' I was in too much turmoil to be glad.

'A little while ago — a week. I did not dare to speak until I was sure it was not some temporary reprieve or a trick of the light.'

'Two months ago you picked my sewing from the floor

That Bad Woman

with as much adroitness as a healthy child. Was it then? Could you see then?'

'Why, yes,' said he. 'I believe that I could perceive a little then. Is the particular date significant?'

My cry burst like shot upon the dead air of the forest. I could hear the wing beats of startled creatures in the trees as I fled, sobbing, back to the house. All the while I had described myself in feminine trickery he had seen me as I was – a fool, and a plain fool. When I achieved the relative sanctuary of our dwelling I managed to compose myself sufficiently to summon Mary and John and informed them that they need make no more special preparations as, by God's grace, the master had regained his sight. I cannot express the dismay I encountered when the servants met my gaze. Humble people have no artifice of expression. 'You knew! You have all been party to my deception.' And then with a sudden running chill like the trickle that pre-empts the flood, a wretched thought crept up on me. 'How long has he had sight?'

'Pardon us, Miss,' said John. 'We are in his paid service and bound to his confidence.'

'And I am mistress of this house,' said I very shakily. 'It is your duty to inform me of the truth.'

In great discomfort they did so. 'He was fully blind when he came to Ferndean. The dark of this place, which ails us all to our bones, served to rest his eyes. His sight was already back before you found him here. He swore us not to say.'

The Secret Diary of Mrs Rochester

I withdrew to a small room at the top of the house that is kept for visitors, although none ever comes. I remained alone until the following day when I consented to see my husband. 'I know all,' I said at once. I must confess that my strongest instinct upon beholding his rueful countenance, now so expressive of his apprehension, was to forgive him and hope that we could commence a normal marriage such as other people have, but he required more than absolution. He was intent upon my understanding. 'You will say now that I tricked you into marrying me, and it is true, but only because I loved you so much that I could run no risk of losing you.'

'It is a queer sort of love,' said I, 'that so lacks trust in its object. It is a corruption of the very soul of that emotion. Commonsense tells me that I should abandon the charade of loving a man who perverts affection's very nature. Yet I persist in believing that beneath your faithless heart is a spirit still hungry for love's redemption. It was that spirit I heard calling to me on that dark night in Morton.'

'Jane, Jane, Jane!' He shook his head and to my annoyance and astonishment I saw that he was close to laughter. 'You adorable idiot. You do not half appreciate the trouble I have taken to woo you. That was not my spirit you heard, but my poor self, travelled three days by carriage and crouched beneath the window on the sodden grass. I learned in the village that Mr Rivers was courting you and deemed it best to win you back by the most dramatic methods. I called to you in a voice so low that only your

That Bad Woman

elf's ears could detect it. When you came to look for me in the garden, I was concealed beneath some shrubbery. There! I have made a clean breast of it. Come and make up to me.'

I do not quite know what was in my mind but when I came close to that erratic giant who had earned my utmost devotion, I felt the whole extent of my humiliation and struck him a violent blow. 'You never loved me,' I cried, 'for love is kind. You only played games with me. At first you pretended that you were to marry Miss Ingrams in order to excite my jealousy. You then dressed up as a fortune-teller, making jackanapes of both Miss Ingrams and myself in order to trick us into revealing our motives while keeping yours well concealed. You disguised from me that you had a wife still living and proposed unlawful marriage to me to trap me into becoming your mistress. Was poor Bertha always mad or did you drive her out of her mind with similar deceptions?'

'Pray do not be hysterical, Jane,' said he very gravely. 'I know that your nerves have been weakened by many trials and that you were subject to fits as a little child, but I warn you to compose yourself.'

'How many more unfortunate women have you thus deceived?' I was beside myself and could not contain my vehemence. 'Was Céline Varens truly the devil you depicted or another poor girl tricked into bigamous marriage?'

His face was aghast as I accused him and I read in his

The Secret Diary of Mrs Rochester

look the unspeakable truth to which my passion had inadvertently given voice. He did not attempt to defend himself but waited until my tirade was at an end and then withdrew with a single utterance: 'You are mad!' A small scratching signified the turning of a key.

There followed the most wretched interlude. The sky grew dark and I was abandoned in that miserable room without a candle, as when I was ten years of age and locked in the red room by Mrs Reed. I do not know how much time passed, whether weeks or months. In that infernal place my one small window showed no light but only the dun talons of an army of trees. I merely know I had much opportunity for introspection and passed the featureless time in contemplation of all that had been wrought upon me and all I had wrought by my own design. Mr Rochester resumed his old bohemian existence and was abroad for some time. When he returned the house remained quiet until that turbulent evening when I was startled by a clatter of hoof beats. I strained at the tiny pane to see if the visitor would be a lady I recognised, or some fresh sacrifice to his vanity to whom he would have to explain the embarrassment of his unstable wife. I could see nothing and was forced to endure the most hideous speculations. To my great surprise I heard footsteps on the stair and when that same personage applied itself to the door it was with a force unknown to any female. The door burst open and there stood my dear cousin, St John Rivers.

That Bad Woman

After a heartfelt reunion he explained that he had been much perturbed by the content of my letters and had prayed for guidance. God had instructed him where his true calling lay and he was now intent on finding out if Mr Rochester had yet another wife alive through bigamous contraction, after which I would be free to go away with him.

Now that the door was open I must make up my mind quickly. In the time of my seclusion I had given much thought to St John and even more to Mr Rochester and arrived at the conclusion that dissolute men, while unreliable and unworthy, have about them an air of tumult that is stimulating to the female sex, and that a woman of virtue has no need of a moral partner, since by her own rectitude is her salvation ensured. Reader, I missed the dear flesh that housed the dark soul. I thanked Mr Rivers for his great kindness but insisted on remaining where I was. After this episode Mr Rochester was very remorseful. He begged my forgiveness and even endeavoured to earn my understanding, insisting that he had never meant to keep me contained, but only assigned me to the attic because my shrewd evaluation of his nature made him fearful of losing me. I disposed of this debate by rendering him senseless with a copper pan.

Since then we have pursued a life of ideal domesticity. I will not pretend that his temperament has altered but I have concluded that human nature is as much God's craft as are all nature's marvels and have curtailed my master's excesses by the simple expedient of keeping his allowance very small, whereby he has learnt the valuable lesson that sin and spending are closely allied. St John, alas, went back to India and died there and Mr Rochester became as useful around the house as any one-armed husband, and as blindly devoted as any tamed beast who comes to accord with the source of all his sustenance.

Perfect Love

◈〜

When the editor of the *Sunday Chimes* told Miss Churchill she was to do a Christmas special on Arabella Cartwheel, the young lady responded by naming twin attributes of the male anatomy wholly unconsidered in the literature of that venerable lady.

The great man was upset. Something about the festive season always brought out his sentimental side. 'It's time for a return to basic values,' he said, quite pleased with this novel concept. 'I want something edifying for my organ.'

He also wanted to teach Miss Churchill a lesson. Gilly Churchill, ace journalist and literary assassin, enjoyed her work too much, making column mince out of celebrities. Arabella Cartwheel, drifting through her tenth decade in a cloud of wilting tulle, had a reputation for being as tough as old toenails. You could rake through the rotting cuttings and find that she danced with a man who danced on the Prince of Wales but, no matter how provoked or

That Bad Woman

confronted, she would continue to smile through her admirably sturdy yellow teeth and talk of what she always talked of – profound and perfect spiritual love.

Gilly chuckled as she quickly prepared a low-calorie meal of Havana cigars. It would come as a surprise to the editor to learn that she was very good with old people. Every Christmas she visited her Aunt Grizel (the one with the dosh). She always brought a bottle of Bailey's Irish Cream. Old people do not drink alone for fear of being labelled alcoholics and bunged in a home. They love to booze and all their gratitude is given to those who facilitate this with their company.

She had been annoyed when the editor disturbed her for she had been feeling organically challenged, having innocently drunk a bottle of mineral water to clear her head of last evening's revels and then, too late, discovered that it was, in fact, a litre of tequila. All the same, she couldn't resist a challenge. Her opponent would be out before the first round and she would be back at her desk by cocktail time.

She chose a little gift for Miss Cartwheel and dressed with care in a gymslip and stilettos. She knew exactly what she wanted. She wanted to confirm that the doyenne of romantic fiction did not actually write her love stories but had a team of zombies chained up in the cellar. She wanted her to boast that she used to be a rattler in the sack (anyone who lasted that long had to be living on someone else's hormones) and most of all she wanted

Perfect Love

to climb so far up her nose that the old lady would tell her to **** off and then she would have the first sentence of her interview: 'I was just a kid looking for a heart-warming Christmas story, but the queen of love told me to **** off.'

The authoress answered the door in full evening regalia.

'You do look wonderful,' gushed Miss Churchill.

'I know.' Miss Cartwheel gave her a jaundiced beam and blinked through two blackened Christmas trees. She swept down the hall in a lampshade of pink gauze.

In fact she felt like hell. For the first time in her life she was suffering from writer's block. For three days she had been stuck on *Never Mind the Bells*. Normally she was aglow with inspiration. Her stories lived with her. From the moment she reached for her eyelashes and her pen and her first cup of ginseng tea, the words flowed like honey . . . *By the time Sir Florian arrived at his beloved Glenfarlow, it was a crimson inferno on the leaden sky. He did not think of his heritage, but only of Willow, trapped in the dungeons* . . . She had been trapped in the flaming dungeons since Friday. By now she would be kippered.

The girl had taken out a notebook and was asking her what had been the biggest influence on her life.

'Profound and perfect spiritual love,' Miss Cartwheel said at once.

'Balls!' The journalist lit up a cigar.

'Indeed!' Miss Cartwheel's face was alight with radiant recall. 'I remember them well. How divinely the young

That Bad Woman

men danced! It was all so beautiful and we were so much in love. In my long and exquisitely happy life I have been fortunate enough to experience the very pinnacle of bliss, which is to love and be loved with a pure heart, for nothing but one's inner self.'

'Let's not beat about the (if you'll forgive the term) bush, Miss Cartwheel,' Gilly said. 'Your ankle tremblers, bustle rustlers, spinster steamers, or whatever you call them, aren't they really the same as my own phenomenally best-selling novel, *Apathy* – tales of man's eternal quest for a spot of how's-your-father?'

'He's dead, thank you.'

'All that surging and churning! Isn't it a metaphor for bonking?'

'I'm afraid I know very little about modern music,' Miss Cartwheel smiled.

'Horizontal jogging, you daft old bat.' The girl bit the end off another cigar and lit it.

'Fie!' Miss Cartwheel was finally nettled. 'I will not have you speak of such things! The word 'jogging' is anathema to me. I cannot imagine why young women should wish to have muscles of steel. Muscles are a manly attribute; women should be soft as kittens – although not, perhaps, as soft as that bulge of thigh showing above your stockings. Those lumpy bits, my dear, are known as cellulite. It is a massing of toxins in the fatty tissues. I would recommend a course of *drainage minceur*.'

Miss Churchill ate her cigar, including the lighted end.

Perfect Love

Arabella Cartwheel watched her with concern. The girl swallowed like an anaconda and then, surprisingly, produced a sweet childish smile. 'We have a lot in common,' she wheedled. 'You have written eleven thousand romantic novels. I have had roughly the same number of gentlemen friends and I can say with absolute authority that not one of them was thinking of profound and perfect spiritual love. Go on, old fruit, admit it. It's a load of rubbish.'

Arabella Cartwheel looked uncomfortable.

'I've got you, haven't I?' Miss Churchill crowed.

Miss Cartwheel nodded reluctantly. 'It's true. I can quite see that you would not inspire profound and perfect love.'

For the first time in her life Miss Churchill was almost speechless. 'You what?'

'It's your eyes, dear. They are the windows of the soul. If the eyes look muddy how can a man see the clear light of the spirit shining through? Your bowels are in crisis! It's the first thing anyone would observe – the yellowish white of eye, the dark circles underneath.'

Miss Churchill was about to rip off her opponent's eyelashes and bash her in the teeth but the old lady had risen like a sprite from her pink velvet sofa and was gone from the room in a whisper of tulle. 'I shall make you a nice cup of senna-pod tea.'

While she was absent Miss Churchill busied herself rummaging in drawers and bookshelves. She found

That Bad Woman

nothing — not even a secret stash of Mars bars. She discovered a giant box of the mauve, violet-scented notepaper for which Miss Cartwheel was renowned. There were vats of vitamins, firkins of fish oil, rafts of royal jelly. She opened one of the containers and sniffed hopefully to see if it might contain gin instead of ginseng. When she was putting it back she accidentally knocked the box of notepaper on the floor. She scooped up the sheets and stuffed them back into the container. Then she saw what had been left behind — a small bundle of yellowing slips of notepaper. Oh, merciful providence! Oh, happy, happy Christmas! A lot of it was soppy tripe. At last she came across the section of correspondence which had been signed 'Shag' and which began, 'My dearest Arab . . .' Miss Churchill chortled horribly as she crouched on the floor to read.

When Arabella Cartwheel arrived with a pot of her evacuating brew, she was still engrossed. 'What are you doing?' the *grande dame* of gush expostulated. 'My private correspondence!'

'Not any more,' Miss Churchill exulted. 'I know all about you now. I know all your little secrets.'

Miss Cartwheel emptied the infusion over her visitor's head. 'Now get out of here, you dirty little faggot,' she said.

The girl stayed where she was, picking what looked like a lot of small black insects out of the turbid liquid that streamed down her face. 'Boo-hoo.'

Perfect Love

'What was that?'

'Boo-hoo, you silly old cow. Can't you see? I'm crying.'

'It is Too Late for Tears.' Miss Cartwheel recited with dignity the title of one of her novels.

'Timeless is My Grief,' Miss Churchill snivelled with gusto. 'My mother – who, er, died in childbirth – left me Her Tears for My Tiara.' She cunningly recalled another of Miss Cartwheel's titles.

'From Where Springs Sorrow?' Miss Cartwheel could not resist flinging in one of her most memorable headings.

Miss Churchill stole a fleeting glance at her hostess's book shelves where all 11,000 of her published titles were ranked. 'From The Groves of Lovelessness,' she uttered on a sigh.

'All the same you were ferreting in my private effects.' Miss Cartwheel made a graceless return to reality. 'You are a thief.'

'A Thief of the Heart?' Miss Churchill essayed hopefully.

'Give me back my letters and get out.'

'Of course, Miss Cartwheel, but first I must explain.' She still held tight to the correspondence. 'You see, I never really believed in love. When you spoke so movingly about the voyages of the heart I just had to find some proof – to see if you were really telling the truth. And now . . .' – she held out the most nauseatingly sentimental of the notes – 'I know you were.'

'I am glad I convinced you. Goodbye.'

That Bad Woman

'Wait!' The girl rose shakily to her feet. She took from her handbag a parcel fetchingly done up in an Oddbins bag. 'A small tribute! Even if I failed to understand the sentiment of your work, I have always been a fan and would like to thank you for the many hours of happiness you have given me.'

Miss Cartwheel unwrapped the parcel and found herself looking at a bottle of fluid roughly the colour of methylated spirits. 'What is it?'

'I chose it specially for you. It's a liqueur. It's called Parfait Amour. It means "Perfect Love".'

The authoress peered closely at the label. 'It's alcohol!' she gasped. 'You know I never drink alcohol. All my life I have kept to my motto: "Lips that touch liquor will never touch mine!"'

'Yes, well you could just pour it in through your nose, you contentious old crow.'

'What did you say?'

'I said, that's why you have a complexion like a rose.'

'There is more to it than abstinence,' Arabella Cartwheel preached severely. 'Every morning I apply a mask of avocado and horse chestnuts. Your own skin, if I may say so, might require some more intensive treatment — a Swabian mud scrub, for instance.' She put out a finger and touched the younger woman's cheek. 'Ah! Perhaps you are already wearing one?'

All her life afterwards Gilly Churchill would congratulate herself on her self-control. 'It isn't really alcohol this,'

Perfect Love

she asserted meekly. 'More a sort of breath freshener. It's a floral tonic – made from violets – the alcohol keeps it from going off. Do try some – just a little swiggy.'

Miss Cartwheel pursed her lips reproachfully.

'Very well then, I'll go.' Gilly held out most of the letters. 'Just answer one more question.'

'If that will send you on your way.'

The hackette batted her opponent playfully with the remaining clump of correspondence. 'Just tell me, who was Shag?'

Arabella Cartwheel looked stricken.

'Why did he want to roll you in the hay? Why did he refer to himself as your stud?'

The queen of hearts cringed. 'Some things are best left alone. That word is not "stud" by the way – it is "steed". The handwriting was always hard to read, but that is understandable.'

Gilly Churchill loomed over her victim. 'Who was he?'

'He was . . . a horse,' Miss Cartwheel said.

'A what?'

'Now you've made me feel silly,' Miss Cartwheel said crossly. 'Shag – otherwise known as Sir Rutland Shag – was my favourite horse. He was a very sensitive animal.'

'A horse that wrote letters?'

'No, of course not, you absurd girl. He merely whinnied his intent. The groom did the actual transcription. His education was frugal and his spelling poor.'

'I don't believe this! It's rubbish!'

That Bad Woman

'Poor child. You don't believe in anything. You are a cynic. It stems from an unhappiness which is all too evident in your hair.'

'My *hair*?'

'Lank tresses, split ends, ne'er helped true lovers make amends!'

Miss Churchill cracked her knuckles. 'You want to know what I don't believe. I don't believe you write all that tosh yourself. It's not possible. I've worked it out. You'd have to have written a novel every two and a half days for the whole of your life to have achieved your output.'

The great novelist did not bat even her exterior set of lashes. 'Unlike the idle little slovens of today, I perfected my speeds in typing when I was a girl. I type 60 words a minute, which is 3,600 words an hour, or 30,000 words a day. As my novels are inspired, I do not have to pause for thought.'

'Pull the other one! What are they inspired by?'

'Profound and perfect . . .'

But the ace journalist had vanished.

After the girl's departure Miss Cartwheel felt disturbed. She was not much disconcerted by her adversary. She frequently had far more invigorating conflicts with her cook. Something else was unsettling her. She did some exercises to the Zsa Zsa Gabor fitness tape and settled at her typewriter with an infusion. Still she could not compose. Sir Florian remained frozen on the moor. Willow was being

Perfect Love

subterraneously sautéed. Perhaps if she had a little swiggy of the floral tonic . . .

She poured a thimbleful, dipped a finger in and tasted it. Delicious! It reminded her of those scented cachous that used to be popular when she was a girl.

Now, who on earth had set fire to Glenfarlow? Why was Willow tied up in the dungeon? She finished off the glass and at once she heard an evil laugh. Of course! It was Sir Rutland Shag. Shag had laughed maniacally when he set Glenfarlow alight. *'Have you ever made love by a roaring fire?' he guffawed as he tied up the hapless Willow.*

She lifted the bottle and swiftly refreshed her throat. A strange energy infused her. The story flowed from enkindled fingers. Never had she written so fluently, so speedily, with such mystical inspiration. She knocked back a half pint of the magic potion and returned to Willow and Sir Rutland in the dungeon. To her surprise, the heroine's bodice had become undone and her bosom was glowing rosily in the light of the flames. *'If I must die, then I must die,' Willow cried piteously, 'but first I should quite like to find out about bonking . . .'*

By midnight the story was ended. It was a masterpiece. Arabella typed a title page for *Never Mind the Bells*, her fingers never faltering until they reached the final noun, where she inadvertently hit an 'a' instead of an 'e'. Her finest novel was finished. The bottle of Parfait Amour had also, mysteriously, been exhausted and Miss Cartwheel felt a little dizzy. She made her way to the bathroom,

That Bad Woman

singing. Her warbling was disturbed by the peremptory return of the entire bottle of liqueur. She peered at the pool of mauve on her marbled tiles. She thought it looked much prettier coming back than all the muesli and yogurt she had kept down over the years. Re-siting her eyelashes and splashing her face with *eau de rose*, she went to make a phone call. Extraordinary that she had forgotten . . .

'Sir Rutland Shag's residence,' said an ancient and exhilarating voice.

'It's Arab,' she enlightened. 'Remember? I've just finished a wonderful novel, and it's almost Christmas. Why don't you come over? Bring a bottle and we'll let our hair down.'

'Mine let me down years ago!' Shag boomed gleefully. 'But everything else is in sporting order.'

Gilly Churchill sat at her typewriter with a mashed avocado on her face. Several times she had crept away to peer in the mirror. She looked terrific – well, nothing that a good night's sleep wouldn't cure. But there was something wrong, a hollow feeling that she could not place. Perhaps she was hungry. She went into the kitchen to look for something nourishing. That was when she found the avocado. She thought about eating it but there are limits to what the human spirit can endure. Still, waste not, want not.

She drank a bottle of Southern Comfort, but it failed to cheer her. She could only envisage the mud it would put

Perfect Love

in her eye. A cup of coffee was what she needed. She decided to go next door and borrow some from her new neighbour.

For several minutes she gazed in silence at the sublime specimen of manhood that responded to her knock, and he gazed back at her. He was the first to break the spell. 'Aargh!' he screamed. 'What do you want?'

She tried to ask for a loan of his Copper Blend but the words kept changing their shape in her mouth. Her bosom heaved and her innards churned. 'I want love,' croaked the creature covered in green slime. 'Profound and perfect, if you know what's good for you.'

The Spirit of the Tree

⚊⚊⚊

Three weeks before Christmas we began counting trees. Crouched in the back of Father's car, forbidden to talk in case we disturbed his concentration as he approached traffic lights, we silently prodded the window, leaving marks that were veined like flies' wings. The flaring V of light in darkened drawing rooms was like a landing strip for the extraordinary event that would descend among us. In that first week there would be only two or three trees, mostly in big houses. The second week there might be eleven or twelve and then on that last Sunday, days before Christmas, they were convened behind windows everywhere – majestic evergreens bedecked like emperors and little crooked shrubs nobbled with lights that were bright and sticky as boiled sweets, a silent community signalling light.

What were they for? Hardly anyone seemed to know. But I knew. The spirit of the tree spoke to Santa Claus,

That Bad Woman

telling him which houses he should visit. The fairy lights were to guide his way. I can't remember where I heard that, but I knew it must be true because it made sense.

We did not understand it then but the atmosphere in those weeks coming up to Christmas, the sense of an unstoppable miracle, was close to the feeling of falling in love. A space was carved in the ordinary world where we were knocked into shape for hard lives ahead, and we could sit in this capsule for a while and be angels or astronauts. We wore a shimmering garment of rapture. Nothing could touch us — not the sharp December air, smelling of fog and frost, not even the curious humpy mood that sat over our parents as we drove home from our grandparents' house. The strange thing was that the happy tension surrounding us children seemed to strike our parents at a different angle and one could not help noticing that as the fairy-lit forests ran riot in suburbia, they grew more and more withdrawn. They reacted to the approach of Christmas as to the onslaught of a war, Mother grimly setting forth for the city to lay in supplies, muttering about the crowds and the price of things, Father swearing as he tacked up the paper accordion decorations, which frequently broke and teasingly drifted, snake-like, through the sombre living room. The biggest ordeal was putting up the Christmas tree. The huge conifer was dragged into the house like a dead bear, then wrestled into an upright position and dumped in a barrel, weighted with bricks. Father would retreat from this

The Spirit of the Tree

engagement, thistled with tiny green needles and looking offended as the tree flooded the house with its pungent green scent.

The small surprise parcels from Santa contained, year after year, the same novelties, the chocolate coins wrapped in foil, an orange. Our parents gave us books, our grandparents biscuits, a tin of sweets and a box of mandarin oranges tricked out like pantomime fairies in tissue and silver paper. Aunt Josie faithfully produced a bottle of Gilbey's Odds-On cocktail for Mother and warm underwear for us girls. Small gifts from far-flung relatives were dangled from the tree or stacked at its base – bath cubes and puzzles and assorted chocolate bars in presentation packs called Selection Boxes. Still, each year, the shock of anticipation was new and when the long (and predictable) day had ended, my last act was always to search the Christmas tree for one unredeemed gift that I might claim for myself and not know its source. As with love, the rapture was always threatened by some small but fatal flaw. There were only two days to Christmas and we still hadn't got our tree.

We never approached any topic directly with our parents. We would either select a crabwise avenue or else open the subject with one parent and allow them to digest it before offering it to the other in a suitable form. Confronted head-on, they reacted like a rabbit caught in a car's headlights. Years later we understood that this was because their responses to everything were so different

That Bad Woman

that it was necessary to find a meeting point before they could offer a united response. Our stark inquisitions were a challenge to their private relationship, the one we would never understand.

'They are selling Christmas trees off in Camden Street,' Celia said.

'That's because they're afraid they won't sell them at all,' Mercy suggested in an offhand way, though you could see the front of her dress twitching over her heart. 'Nearly everyone has one already.'

'When are we getting ours?' I burst out unwisely.

Mother stood up and began clearing away the plates, although we were still toying with our macaroni cheese. Father held on to his plate and slowly finished eating the wormy-looking pile. He glanced out the window, where the early afternoon had already flung up steel-grey shutters, and then, as if making a comment on the weather, he mildly observed, 'There will be no Christmas tree.'

There was a brief, somersaulting pause and Celia and Mercy began to laugh. Father often made jokes and he kept a very serious face when he did. I had not yet got the hang of humour. I started to cry. Mother raced in to rescue me and Father slapped both hands down on the table. 'There will be no Christmas tree! No turkey, no presents, no nonsense!' He said this angrily but immediately he looked sorry and added in a gentler voice, 'We are in a bad way. We owe money. We must all pull together. It is only one other day in the year.'

The Spirit of the Tree

We all sat perfectly still at the table until at last Father got up and went out. '*We* don't owe money,' Celia said.

'He has to sell the car.' Mother sounded shaken. 'He's going to have to make do with a bicycle.' She didn't mention any privations that might have affected herself. Women didn't. She did not tell us – and it was years before we found out – that he had lost his job six months previously and they had been trying to live in a normal way in the hope that something else would turn up, and nothing had, except bills. All she said was that there was a tin of pineapple in the press and she would make a pineapple cake for tea.

Mercy, at eight, was an elfin little girl with white-blonde hair that made her look unnaturally pale, but now she seemed completely drained of colour. 'They have cancelled Christmas,' she said when we were alone.

'They can't cancel Christmas,' Celia said. 'It happens anyway. Santa comes anyway.'

'But Santa only comes if you have a tree in your window.' My voice rose in dawning horror. 'That's how he knows which houses to visit.'

'We'd better go and say a prayer,' Celia said. 'We'll go to the church and light a candle.'

The senior saints with their long robes and long faces offered no hope. They were greedy for suffering and would tell us, if they could (as grown-ups tended to), that

That Bad Woman

sacrifice was an opportunity to add jewels to our crown in heaven. We knelt in front of the crib. Surely children everywhere wanted the same things.

On the way home it was so dark the Earth seemed to have gone out. Only the bright arrowheads of Christmas trees lit the world. Despairingly, we counted the trees. Everyone had one. Even our own prim street was ablaze with colour. Even the old Misses Parker had one. I had streaked ahead of the older girls and was reaching for their knocker before they had time to stop me. 'What are you doing?' they gasped. But the elderly sisters, who were Quakers and famously charitable, had already opened their door. I told them our father could not afford a Christmas tree and that Santa would not come to our house if he did not see the fairy lights. At once they agreed that we should have their tree and even carried it down the road with its decorations tinkling and light flexes trailing. Mother was confused, but she accepted the tree with thanks and left it propped up in the hall. We spent the afternoon stroking the cold silver strands of tinsel that the Misses Parker had threaded through its branches and that felt like mermaids' hair.

A couple of hours later Father was to be seen striding down the street, the stiffly bedecked tree clasped in his arms like a war missile. We ran behind him, picking up small ornaments as they clopped off onto the frosty pavement and trying furtively to get around him to retrieve those decorations that belonged to us. The Misses Parker

The Spirit of the Tree

eyed him with hateful sympathy as he told them we had no need of charity.

Mercy and I looked to Celia. She was the eldest so she had to do something and she had to do it before that first, fatal leaching of faith, after which Christmas would never seem the same again. 'It's all right,' she said. 'We don't need the grown-ups. We'll get our own Christmas tree.'

'Where, Cee?'

'How?'

She went out alone the following day. We waited for her, watching behind the drawing-room window. When she came home she looked small and cold, her face pinched with anxiety, her hands dug deep in her pockets.

'Have you got it?' we pestered her, although we could see nothing.

She took her hand out of her pocket and showed a small, greenish pine cone. 'I found this,' she said. 'We'll grow our own tree.'

'But that will take years,' I complained.

'Then we'd better do it right now,' she said in her practical way.

There was one apple tree in the garden, a thin forsythia and, in spring, a clump of wallflowers. There was a forgotten region, which had become a compost heap of leaves and trimmings and pruned branches. Celia instructed us to clear away the rubbish so that we could dig a hole for the Christmas tree. Gingerly we dipped in our mittened hands and began to lift the bits of half-burnt refuse and piles of dead leaves and old potted plants, layered up over some more substantial hulk. Whatever this was, you could tell that its personality remained intact, like a man preserved in a bog for a thousand years. Desiccated fingers pointed up at the sky. We pulled away more rubbish to discover a beautiful shape, like the skeleton of a leaf.

It looked like some old fish that had been nibbled dry so that only its bare bones and its scaly spine poked out. It looked like the rusted hulk of a ship that had sunk many years ago and its barnacled frame endured. It did not look like – but definitely was – a Christmas tree. Triumphantly, we hauled it out. Some of its branches were broken, but it had been a good tree once, before it was cast out after festive service in some better year. And it was ours. We had found it.

'It's a bit brown,' Mercy mentioned, reluctant to criticise.

'We'll make it green,' Celia said.

She had learnt a thing in school, to make leaves for bare branches from crepe paper. We had sixpence between us and bought two packets of the dark-green, bark-rough stuff, with its wrinkles and its rustle of theatre. We cut it into long strips and wound them round the branches, Sellotaping the ends, until the entire frame was bandaged in green. Then Mercy, who was the artistic one, made fringed strips and taped these along the branches to look like needles. Bumping it forward in little steps, we managed to get the tree into the house and leaned it inside the window. It looked magnificent.

The Spirit of the Tree

There was an anxious moment when Father came home and discovered the mummified horticultural corpse. He was frowning. He seemed to be thinking. When he spoke, his voice sounded strange, as if he was getting a cold. 'It's all right,' he said. He bent to stroke our hair in the cautious way that we had stroked the silver mermaids' hair on the Misses Parker's tree. 'I think,' he said, 'it will be all right.'

From then on, everything proceeded as normal. Two big boxes were brought down from the attic, one with lights and one with ornaments. Father plunged his arms into the entrails of frayed wiring and the fairy lights clinked in an insouciant way like china teacups as he tried to unsnarl them. Then for hours he was up on a ladder, locked into some intimate contest, cajoling and cursing, beseeching and loathing, muttering strange, enticing, sulphurous words so that Mother had to drag us away, while the lights twittered and wavered and at last responded to his male authority. Tinsel ornaments twinkled with magical depths. Carnival colours bumped off every sober surface in the room and, in the window, the lights shimmered enticingly. I couldn't sleep that night and at dawn I crept out onto the landing to see if Santa had come. I was worried about the spirit of the tree. It might have grown faint in its old parcelled trunk. In the back of my mind too I had begun to wonder if any part of Christmas could survive now that our parents had no money, if in some way every single thing that came to us must not

That Bad Woman

begin and end with them. Santa's parcels were there. I couldn't resist it and began tearing mine open right away, crying out with pleasure as the familiar objects came into view. From his bedroom came Father's voice, a weary growl: 'Get back to bed or I'll take the whole blasted lot away from you.'

After a fearful pause, Celia called back bravely, 'They are not your property!'

There was even a turkey. Father had won it in a raffle. It was a dinosaur-like creature, its languidly naked form looking like something that ought to be clothed. While we composed a jigsaw puzzle at the base of our tree, we could hear Mother's anguished voice from the kitchen: 'Get into the oven, you big bastard!'

My sisters have related this incident to their children and they think it is a sad story but for the three of us it remains our best Christmas ever. It was the year we made Christmas happen. Perhaps it would have happened anyway. Our grandparents and Auntie Josie came, the monstrous bird was finally cooked and consumed and everyone fell asleep. As usual, last thing, I checked the tree, walking around its mysteriously rustling branches, examining its paper folds to see if anything had been left behind. Nestling in the elbow of a branch was a tiny package wrapped in red and tied with gold tinsel thread. I unlooped it and slowly peeled back the paper. Inside was a little enamel box with a black cat painted on its front,

The Spirit of the Tree

framed in blue flowers. I opened the box and it was filled with doll-sized fruit pastilles coated in sugar. As I slipped it into my pocket my heart dipped in that perfect curve that lovers experience when they know, against all odds, the rewards of reckless faith.

Confession

The two girls ran between the aisles. They had a penny which they had decided to invest. They would light a candle and pray for Uncle Matt to come and visit, because he always gave them a shilling. They slowed down as they passed a pew which was full of people who shuffled on their knees to fill the gap left when a man stepped off the end and vanished into a box.

'Where did he go?' Betty said to Fanny. Fanny did not know so she told Betty not to speak in church. Betty turned her attention to a kneeling woman whose bowed head was wrapped in a scarf. 'What's in there? Why is everyone going in there?' She clutched the carved end of the pew in case Fanny would drag her away. Her face was level with the kneeling woman's head which rose so slowly that there was a moment when Betty feared that the scarf might not actually contain a face.

That Bad Woman

'It's the confession box,' she told Betty. 'We go in there for forgiveness.'

'Forgiveness for what?' Betty said.

'For when we have been wicked,' the woman smiled.

'What's wicked?' Betty said as Fanny dragged her away.

'She is. She eats children,' Fanny told her.

'You'd go to jail for that,' Betty said hopefully.

Fanny held her sister's hand. She lit the taper and touched a candle and the wick curled and sizzled and a black straggle of smoke grew out of it and then a bright eye of flame blazed and gazed at them. 'No one ever finds out,' Fanny whispered. 'She eats every bit of them, first the fingers and the eyes and then she nibbles off all the flesh. By then she is too full to stand so she sits down and belches to make some room and then one by one she crunches the bones. Last of all she eats the hair, holding it up and licking the strands off her fingers.'

The moment she had said this Fanny forgot about it, but for years afterwards Betty woke in the night to the muffled eager munching of bones, and then she would see the woman's face and have to watch her eating the hair, which waved and straggled like the black smoke on the candle. The woman had had black hungry eyes that burned into Betty and when she smiled she showed long, bone-crunching teeth, and the red on her lips made a saw pattern in the wrinkles, as if the blood dripped down.

By now Fanny was going to confession. She had to take Betty because she had to take her everywhere, and

Confession

Betty was made to kneel beside her in the line. When other people emerged they looked subdued but Fanny always came out smiling. She held her joined hands over her face so that people would not see, but Betty saw and once or twice she noticed her licking her lips.

'What happens when you go in there?' Betty said.

'It's a secret,' Fanny told her. 'I'm not allowed to say.'

The younger sister became obsessed with the confession box and pestered Fanny, pulling at her skirt or poking her in bed at night so that Fanny at last had to relent. 'Well, then, I will tell you if you promise never to mention this to another living soul. Behind the door there is a smaller door and beyond that a great big room with a party going on. There is a long table with cake and ice cream and jelly and meringues. Every person who goes in can eat as much of everything as they like. I had three meringues.' Betty was five and it would be two more years before she could go to confession and each week Fanny added more and more enticing details. Once she took a silver-wrapped sweet from her pocket and handed it to her sister. 'I saved you that.' And every Saturday when she left Betty in the pew, shivering with envy, she told the priest, 'I lied.'

When Betty's turn finally came her whole life was dominated by the ordeal. In school she was prepared for her first confession. It was revealed to her that Christ had died for her sins. 'What sins?' she said in terror, but it was a bottomless pit, an unending menu written by the devil. She

That Bad Woman

supposed that sin would come naturally to her now that she had reached the age of reason, but soon she came to realise that like long division, it would remain forever a puzzle. 'Bless me, Father, but I have no sins,' she said. The priest was full of contempt and wanted to know how every man on earth was a sinner but she alone was above reproach. She was introduced to some invisible and unpleasant part of herself called a conscience and compelled to examine it, employing a litany of the seven deadly sins, from which flowed all iniquity; pride, covetousness, lust, anger. She knew she did not possess the extreme emotions necessary for such passionate-sounding weaknesses. At night she lay awake trying to imagine ways in which her thoughts or actions might be sinful, but when she produced some sins they sounded too evil and the priest's breath was drawn in in revulsion. She often had to tell the same ones because she couldn't think of any others and it seemed that even in the dark she was recognised, for the confessor would demand, 'Am I right in thinking you were in here before asking to be forgiven for the selfsame acts of badness? You are turning out very degenerate.'

In desperation she would come to confession half an hour early and inspect all the boxes. The confessors' names were inscribed in gold on a wine-coloured plaque above the door and she always hoped that there might be a new one. Sometimes in the dark, while the priest was censuring her, she felt with her fingers the grainy wall of the box, hoping to encounter a little latch or catch that

Confession

would spring open the door to the big room with the party. The confession box was constructed like a moth, with a solid central part where the priest wielded mercy behind dusty curtains and on either side of him were spread out two sections like wings where one sinner waited and one confessed. While she waited Betty could hear the murmured vices of other sinners and the priest's disillusioned drone of pardon but Fanny always came out smiling behind her hands and still Betty imagined that beyond the old priest, waiting like a spider to dissect your rotting soul, the room waited, the long table set with the devil's unending menu – the jellies only half eaten, the meringues bloated with sweetened cream.

The two girls grew up. Fanny was a striking, spiky young woman, around whom jealous feuds broke out among men who had not even known they liked her. Betty was a soft, shy, pretty girl, who blushed and who was enraptured by romance. Into the dark, musty confession box they brought the fragrance of young women and the provocation of other men's lust. The dim, coffin-like space grew tropical with the scent of their hair and their breathless whispers of tentative carnal celebration. Gone was the pastor's dolorous drone. He quizzed them eagerly, relentlessly. Fanny enjoyed these sessions.

'*Where did he touch you?*'

'On my breasts. My thighs. On my . . .!' And she stopped and gave a little gasp, as if remembering.

'*Was his mouth open when he kissed you? Did you touch his*

That Bad Woman

private parts? Did you? Did he put it between your legs? Did he waste the seed?'

When Betty entered the box, even before she opened her mouth, the priest appeared half demented with rage. She often let boys go a little bit far because it seemed kind and anyway it was no harm for she had made up her mind that she would not get around to actual sex until she was married. These physical interludes passed in a kind of pleasant blur that stopped her thinking about them too much except when she went to confession and the priest forced her to articulate all the pleasant acts of tenderness in a way that made them appear vulgar and brutal and, in a particularly revolting way, caused her to feel that she was being forced to do them all over again but against her will. There came a time when she knew that she must never, ever do them again. She still dressed invitingly and made little mews when she was kissed and blushed and flapped her eyelids until her suitors were beside themselves and then she seemed to turn to ice. Betty was miserable. She hated being mean to boys and when they called her a tease she felt she was turning out like Fanny, disclosing a feast to which they were not invited. One man told her it was her own fault for driving men crazy and he raped her and then he strangled her. He was haunted by the look upon her face which was a look of recognition and, almost, a look of gratitude. The thing Betty finally understood was that she had known all along that this would happen and now, at last, she need no longer dread it.

Confession

Fanny got married and everyone breathed a sigh of relief. She had a routine sort of life except for a restless phase about ten years after that. There was something on her mind and she was tormented by an urge to tell her husband. She knew the kindest thing was to say nothing but it was like a thorn in her system and sooner or later it was going to have to work its way out. 'I've been having an affair,' she said to him one night when he wanted to sleep and she wanted to make love.

'Who with?' he said, and she told him it was his friend, his best friend, the man who had been like a brother to him since childhood, whose company he preferred to anyone else's.

There was a period of unpleasantness with accusations and denials, and in the end the two men never spoke to each other again but that was none of Fanny's business. The only thing that concerned her was to confess properly, before God, who has the power to wipe away all sins. She had not been to confession since Betty's death. The brown box looked small and quaint now, like a music box left over from childhood and stored in the attic, and for a moment she felt foolish, but for all Catholics there comes a time when they need to feel once more the pleasant abrasion of total cleansing so she went inside and bent her bony knees and put her dry red lips up to the little wire grill and told the priest, 'I lied.'